'Conditioned for Freedom'

Ernest Dyer

www.newgeneration-publishing.com

New Generation Publishing

Chapter One

The muted taping on the steamed-up side window of the campervan took John by surprise just as he was about to prepare his dinner while parked in the car-park of a small low-budget hotel adjacent to the A47 Norwich bypass. On sliding open the door he saw a lightly dressed young women, striking long blond hair, clear blue eyes, and bare feet on what was a very cold, very wet, evening.

'I need a hug, can I have a hug please' she pleaded.

John's initial reaction was to reach out, but he checked himself as he remembered the recent well-publicised issues with men being accused of assaulting women. There was also the possibility that she was accompanied by one or more men waiting in the shadows to emerge and accuse, with blackmail or even robbery in mind. All these reservations crumbled when he saw a depth of sadness and fear in the woman's eyes.

He stepped down from the van and took both of her hands into his own. He could feel just how cold she was as he guided her into the van to one of the comfortable seats in the back.

She was now sobbing and shivering, and John reassured her that she was safe and that he would do what he could to help in what must be a difficult situation for her. As he heated the kettle, and turned the van heating to full, he felt it best to pause and let her feel more at ease before they started talking about whatever was troubling her.

Having served up a strong and heavily sugared mug of tea and offering a packet of biscuits he sat opposite the woman and gently prompted her to talk.

'My name is Janina and my recent life has been one of imprisonment, as a bride in waiting to an evil man'.

Now John picked up on the women's eastern-European accent as she went on to outline a story of being in effect trafficked from her Lithuanian homeland.

'My name is John......just begin your story from whenever you think it would be appropriate.'

'Thank you John......this time last year I was so happy to graduate from Vilnius University with a good degree in quantity surveying. I was fine living with my parents in our small flat in the Vilnius suburb of Naujoji Vilnic. Even though the area is now pretty much a post-industrial wasteland of abandoned factories and bleak blocks of low-rent flats. At least there is a residual sense of community as neighbours exchange their sadness at change and their hopes for their children and grandchildren.

But work in my qualified area of surveying was scarce in my country. I applied for many jobs across Lithuania and the neighbouring Baltic countries, but no success. Just to get by I took a job in a bookshop in the old-town centre of the City which, although poorly paid, was quite enjoyable. I felt comfortable being surrounded by a wide range of books that I could spend much of the day browsing. And the access to so many imported novels written in English provided the incentive for me to improve on my high-school level English.

From time to time a fashionably dressed young women would breeze into the shop, slowly peruse the shelves and usually buy a book. As we became more familiar our brief casual conversations progressed from observations about such topics as the weather or the political situation to more personal exchanges about what we had been 'up to' recently, or how we intended spending a coming weekend, and similar exchanges.

During these I had mentioned my narrow social life being primarily due to a lack of income and with most of my old friends having gotten married or moved abroad. After a couple of months the women, named Lina, came into the bookshop just before closing time and on approaching the counter to pay for a book, our eyes met and we shared a kindly furtive smile at an old man in front of her who had been fumbling about in a purse for the correct coins to complete a modest purchase. When I had wrapped and passed Lina her book she suggested we go out for a coffee and cake at a nearby cafe.

Once at the cafe, settled into our window seats, and having been served coffee and chocolate cake, Lina began to tell me about a friend who was living in London doing really well working in property development. Apparently, her company was intending to expand but was short of surveyors Lina laughingly suggested that I might be interested in moving to London.

As our conversation moved on to discuss a recently released James Bond film being shown at the local cinema, I was taking in the view from the broad windows of the cafe. This took in a dismal section of a main street along which the winter's ice-cold wind blew litter up the roadway, some of which collected against the prone bodies of a number of homeless rough sleepers, attempting to shelter as they huddled in the doorways of shabby boarded-up shops.

Whilst taking this in I could also imagine how different London would be – the smart people, colourful street scenes, a level of prosperity being obvious. If not 'paved with gold' then the streets of London certainly seemed to offer prospects unavailable in Lithuania.

We parted that evening, but our coffee and cake meetings became a regular occurrence, and we would occasionally follow this with a trip to see a movie. One time Lina laughingly took my picture insisting that I should let my long hair free of the slide-contained bundle I had tucked under my old woollen hat.'

Just then John saw Janina freeze, her eyes wide and her small hands whitening as she gripped the edge of her seat. A powerful motorbike was swinging into the car-park, its headlight arching as its light swept cross the van's wide windscreen. The heavily built driver wore a distinctive gold helmet. He and the pillion rider got off the bike, lifted the heavy machine easily onto its stand, and made towards the hotel entrance. John immediately decided that these two were ex-military. If perhaps a bit heavier than they would have been when serving, they still moved forward purposefully and were obviously scanning the area as they walked.

'They are looking for me, they are very bad men whispered a trembling Janina, and they will hurt you badly if I am found here.'

John passed over his phone.....'I am going to see what they are up to. You take this and allow me five minutes from the time I enter the hotel, if I am not back by then phone the police as an emergency and then lie down on the floor of the van behind the front seats.'

His calmness surprised Janina but something about his assertively calm demeanour allowed her abject fear to ease into more just intense anxiety.

John left the van by the sliding side door and swiftly made his way across the rain-soaked car-park towards the hotel until, crouching at the shadowed side of the doorway, he had a clear view into the reception area.

What he saw was one of the men at the reception desk and the other with his back to the entrance idly looking at a framed poster on the wall. The one at the desk was now arguing quite loudly with the male receptionist and John could hear him shouting.

'Give me the fucking guest book.'

The receptionist reached for the phone, but he was grabbed roughly by the collar and dragged across the desk. John casually walked into the reception area innocently asking.

'Is something wrong, do you need a first-aider?'

The second man turned to him, put his hand on John's chest and said.

'You had best get fucking lost mate'.

John stepped back as if to leave and the man began to turn away, as he did so John grabbed his hand, pulled the man off balance and hit him hard in the small of his back, as he fell he swung round to face John whose second blow caught the man full under the chin sending him reeling back. By now the first man had let the receptionist go and was coming towards John, drawing a stiletto knife from his leather jacket.

Now John felt a surge of excitement, sensing his own military training co-ordinating his movements. Although outweighed by his opponent, John was significantly quicker on his feet and he aimed a sweeping kick to the side of the man's head just as he lunged forward with the knife. As his opponent fell John grabbed his wrist and in a flowing motion forcefully twisted and jerked it back, an action rewarded with the satisfying crack of the wrist-bone. The knife dropped to the floor and the man was on his knees in obvious pain but still able to swear loudly at John.

'Call the police,' John said to the receptionist as he quickly left the hotel.

On his way back across the car-park John paused by the motorbike, leaning over to rip off the plastic tube running from the petrol tank to the carburettor.

Once back in the van he told Janina that he had neutralized the heavies but that they should probably move on.

'Yes,' she said. 'I could see something of the fighting through the glass doors and they or others will soon be after me, and now you. They badly want something that I have and now they will also want revenge. They always inflict harm, they don't expect to suffer it.'

As the van turned out into the main road John glanced into the rear-view mirror and could see one of the now injured motorcyclists using his phone to take a picture of the van even as he was leaning heavily against the door of the hotel.

More reassuringly, John also passed an oncoming police car just turning into the hotel car-park. Well that should keep them busy for a while as they try to explain their injuries and the threatening behaviour towards the receptionist he thought.

'What now?' asked Janina.

'I think you should just drop me off at the nearest railway station, I will try to get to Dover and across the channel and hitch-hike across Europe and home – those men and others they work with are seriously bad.

They work within a London-based drug-dealing network headed by an evil man – my future husband!'

'I am thinking that the marriage has just been called off....and we will not be parting company, at least for the time being.' Said John

The surge of energy that has been running through John's body and mind during the past 10-15mins had made him feel alive 'again'. The reason he was in Norfolk was to arrange for the sale of a wooden sailing boat he kept at a boatyard on the Norfolk Broads. He had been parked in the unlit corner of the hotel car-park just to make some dinner and get a couple of hours sleep before heading back to London.

He had been feeling a mild form of depression, becoming increasingly more oppressive as the time since his leaving the Metropolitan Police Force lengthened - The prospects of early retirement had initially looked good and working in his brother's office supply company was reasonably paid and the work was quite routinely easy.....but this did not compare when following 24 years of relative excitement. First serving in the Marines for 10 years then 14 in the police with the last 6 in the Special Firearms Unit (SOC19) seconded to the Counter Terrorism Command (SO15).

His current working life had lacked something and now he had a gift, an opportunity to experience the sense-tingling excitement of danger, a danger that at least still seemed to be relatively manageable – dealing with thugs rather than military opposition.

Throw in 'a maiden in distress' and he could only see the situation in terms of good fortune rather than bad luck, of challenge rather than stress. He wasn't to know that he would soon learn that the 'maiden in distress' label, apart from reflecting his age, was also to be something of a misjudgement.

They swung round the Acle A47 roundabout and headed toward the seaside town of Great Yarmouth. John asked Janina if she had a mobile phone, and when she confirmed this he said.

'Then that was probably how they traced you to the hotel.....give it to me.'

One of the large high-sided lorries that transported the roots of the locally grown sugar beet crop to the processing factory at Cantly by the River Yare was passing the other way and John threw the phone into the back of it.

The ten mile route to Great Yarmouth took them along an almost straight two-lane road with a short gentle curve at about five miles. On their right-hand side was low-lying farmland through which trains passed (or rather rattled) along the somewhat neglected single-track line that ran from Norwich to the coastal town. Beyond the elevated track lay the wide expanse of Breydon Water. On the other side the farmland continued, but within about one hundred metres of the road the marshy farmland gave way to extensive reed beds. And although darkness obscured the reeds themselves John could smell their mild scent as they swayed in the gentle breeze. These were the thin, but tough, hollow-stemmed reeds used to thatch so many north Norfolk cottages.

As they sped along John was planning the next step. He still needed to know more about Janina and her situation, but this could wait until they had found a safe place to stay for the night.

By the time they reached the bridge over the River Bure on the outskirts of the town, John had at least formulated a plan for that night. Turning left he skirted the built-up central area and within ten minutes he drew into a campsite (sited beside Great Yarmouth Race Course) that he knew catered for the type of short stays favoured by touring caravans and motor homes, so ideal for his relatively small VW Campervan.

After signing in and paying for a pitch at the camp reception and having purchased a tooth-brush and some shower gel for Janina in the small site-shop, they cruised slowly around the campsite and found a fairly quiet spot in a corner of the extensive site.

As they left the reception John noticed a hand-chalked sign indicating that a mobile fish and chip van will be coming to the site that evening, suggesting an easy meal for later.

It did not take long for them to be parked up and connected to the site electricity, and within the hour John had also been able to log on to the internet. He had already decided to pick up Janina's story after they had eaten and were more at ease with each other.

It was 10 o'clock before they had eaten their fish and chip supper. The food was somewhat of a novel experience for Janina who explained that the common meals in Lithuania were, for most less affluent people, limited to versions of beetroot soup, bean-based stews, cheap fish or pork patties, pickled or smoked fish, then only very occasionally a modest amount of pork and chicken. Even accepting that the range of food available had increased since the breakup of the Soviet Union in 1988, and the subsequent closer relationship between Lithuania and Western Europe and the Scandinavian countries.

'The fish in crisp batter, and chips with vinegar were quite tasty and have filled me up nicely,' said Janina.

'Mind you, I haven't eaten since having a banana at breakfast, so I was very hungry.'

'Right' said John. 'You go over to the shower-block and get ready for the night while I prepare the beds.'

As he watched her walking over to the shower-block John observed how easily she moved, even if she did appear to be continuously glancing around as if expecting to be challenged. He also reminded himself that he was 15-20 years older than Janina and had eased into becoming quite a confirmed bachelor who would now find it difficult, perhaps impossible, to form a relation beyond the occasional 'relief-seeking' short-term encounter.

It did not take John long to transform what were van seats during the day into two single beds for the night. Once he had drawn the full curtains that enclosed the sleeping area and switched the lighting from the main overhead light to two subdued night-lights, the van seemed nicely cosy. He spread his sleeping bag on the bed intended for Janina and the spare blanket on his own.

By 10.30 p.m. John had also washed and had opened two bottles of beer, offering one to Janina as he invited her to continue with her outline of recent events.

Janina wiped her hand across her lips to clear a smooth line of beer foam and picked up her story.

'Well.... Lina and I continued to meet up for coffee and cake and the occasional trip to the cinema. And she did sometimes mention London and what a successful career and enjoyable time her friend was having. Then one rainy Monday about two months since we had begun to build a friendship I arrived at work to be met by a serious looking shop owner, Christian, who said that business continued to be poor and that he had very reluctantly decided that I would have to go. It had been pretty clear that the bookshop was struggling. I had been able to read about a book a week whilst working and had managed to read through many of the 'western classics'. Dickens, Dostoevsky, and Dumas, just to note some of the Ds.

And my English had improved in 'leaps and bounds' as your quaint English saying goes. With a week's pay in my pocket (a mere 250 litas) I left the bookshop and wandered down the street in something of daze. Wondering how I could manage and avoid being a burden on my mumeda, mum in English and my tevalis, dad in English, who I knew were struggling to get by on a small pension.

I was feeling pretty low, a mood accentuated by the shabby street scene, its economic disadvantage was obvious, not least in the number of boarded-up shops and even in the clothes and the demeana of most of the people I passed. Then I heard my name called, it was Lina calling from across the street. She quickly crossed over and I fell into her arms and burst into tears. She held me tight as my stream of tears eased into more gentle sobs. 'Come on let's hurry to the cafe and you can share your woes with me over strong coffee and sticky chocolate cake.'

Janina paused to take a drink from her bottle of beer, then said to John.

'I am sorry I don't suppose that you want to listen to all this detail. But going through all the steps leading by to my being here at this campsite with you on a cool English summer's evening is helping me to make sense of what has been happening.'

'That's fine,' said John. 'You just take your time and go into as much detail as you feel comfortable with.'

Thank you…. so once settled into the cafe I told Lina what had happened to my job and my concerns about the future, one with no immediate job prospects and one in which I did not want to become a burden on my parents.

She simply asked me if I would like to go to London. She said that we could go together and that she was sure that her friend would put us up and help us to get work……that it will be an adventure for us. She brushed aside my objections about travel costs and living expenses. She said that she would take care of this and asked me to imagine the two of us arm in arm strolling along the famous Oxford Street as we brush off one young man after another seeking our attention.

Now I was joining in her laughter and the miserable mood of earlier had lifted, it seemed that I had a future to look forward too.

Within a week I had sorted out travel documents, packed a small suitcase and was at Vilnius airport having cleared departures and was queuing to board a plane. Just then I heard Lina say a cheerful hi to a tall male standing behind us in the queue. He was quite tough looking, with close cropped greying hair and a scar down his right cheek. He greeted Lina and said it was good to see her. Once we had boarded this guy, Florin, sat down on the isle-side of our row of three seats. We were introduced and, whilst I was curious about such a co-incidence of his being known to Lina and then also being sat next to us, I felt it best to just accept the situation. During the flight Lina kept very quiet which was so out of her normally bubbly character.

I just assumed that she was nervous about flying. But I was really enjoying the experience – the first time I had flown – at times flying above the cloud cover with the sunlit clouds stretched out like a giant fluffy white duvet, and the times when the sky was clear I was in awe at the vast landscapes, of forest, farmland, and coastline, set out below.

On landing at Heathrow, Florin took charge and Lina accepted this. In the arrival hall we were joined by another tough looking individual this one, given his being black, was more obviously English. Florin indicated that we should follow the greeter and that they would drop us off in central London. We were led into the car-park and to a large black Mercedes. I was surprised that Florin opened the front passenger door for Lina and indicated that I should take a rear seat, he then got in beside me.

Within 30 mins I caught a first glimpse of Wembley Football Stadium then the Alexander Palace, both of which I had seen on Lithuanian T.V. The car turned into a side road and drew to a halt. Lina began to get out of the car, and I was beginning to feel unsettled and asked what was happening. Now with one leg out of the car she turned towards me and with tears running down her cheeks said. 'I am so sorry Janina'.

Now I was frightened and tried to get out of the car. Florin grabbed my wrists and looking directly into my eyes he calmly told me that I was in effect a prisoner and that if I cooperated with them I would be safe but if not, I would be hurt quite badly.

We continued on our journey east across the city passing Euston, St Pancras, and then Kings Cross stations, where we turned right into what seemed to be quite a rundown road from which we turned right into a short road leading to what a street sign noted as Argyle Square.

We drew up outside a large terraced house with a dimly lit notice indicating that it was the 'Argyle Hotel' and I could see that the Hotel included a shabby terraced house on each side of the main one. As we drove around the Square, I noticed a number of girls sitting or standing in small groups at the entrance to some of the houses.

I was hustled up the steps leading to a pretty dirty reception area with a rat-like man at the counter and on the wall behind him a somewhat faded poster showing Buckingham Palace.

My new companions led me up to the third floor and showed me into a large room with a bed, table, an armchair, a T.V. set on the wall and a door leading to a small toilet and shower-room.

Florin said that I was to remain there – that my food would be brought up to me and that I was to strip naked and put on a dressing gown that he took from the back of the door. He again warned me that no-one knew where I was, the windows were sealed, and the door would be locked with his colleague seated on the other side.

I asked him why I was being treated in such a way and he indicated that I should sit down and, standing over me, he said that one way or another my life had changed quite dramatically. If I did what I was told I will have a comfortable material life. But that if I did not cooperate then I would be severely beaten, then one of them, probably him, will strangle me and that my body would be dumped into the River Thames, to flow on the tide to the estuary and out into the sea. Expressing no emotion at all he said 'Janina will be no more. It is as simple as that.'

John could see that she was now quite upset as she relived that awful experience, so he said. 'Let's take a break Janina, have another beer and try to relax.'

'Yes, I will have another beer please John, but I do want to at least try to get to the end of my story tonight. You should know what I have been through so that you will be able to clearly understand the difficult, indeed very dangerous, situation, that have got yourself involved in......I was so frightened, that I striped off and got into bed, still confused about what awaited me – this was a very different London to the one I had imagined.

It was about an hour later that the door was unlocked and Florin and another man came into the room. The sight of this second man made me shudder. He was quite tall, but it was his sheer bulk that made him so imposing. I would guess he was aged somewhere between 40 and 50, with clearly dyed black hair, some gold teeth, tiny eyes, and a large fleshy mouth, with a neck that even bulged over his open-necked shirt. My thought was of a villain from a James Bond film but no, he was more than just an onscreen character.......standing in front of me was a man who I can only say exuded evil.'

'Get up and take the dressing gown off' said Florin – my natural reaction was to pull the dressing gowned tighter, but he just reached out and pulled it from me. I stood naked in front of these two men. The large man – Ashif Rahman - ordered Florin from the room and told me to stand up tall and to slowly turn around. After I had done this twice, he reached out to run his hand through my hair. 'Beautiful' he said, 'you are what I have been seeking, are you a virgin?' I was so nervous and blurted out that I had had one intimate relationship whilst at university.

'In that case he said our marriage will have to wait for a period for you to reclaim your virginity, if via a plastic surgeon, and of course for you to study the Koran and convert to Islam.'

He then left the room and a woman came in with my dinner on a tray. This was a women – Kay – who was to be my companion, she would ensure that I had all of the clothes, toiletries, and anything else I required. Kay would be someone who I was to get to know quite well. She told me to finish my dinner and to try to sleep and that and we will talk in the morning – She said that she was not entirely sure what was going to happen to me but she did have some idea and that, for sure, I was not going to end up in one of the brothels on the square, unlike many other girls that spent their first night in London at this seedy hotel.

Although it had been a long day I found it difficult to get to sleep, so many questions were running through my head......who were these men, why did Lina my assumed friend lead me into their hands, but most of all I was fearful of what my future held. I did eventually manage to get some sleep, waking about 7 o'clock to sunlight streaming through the dirty window, on the broad sill of which two scruffy pigeons were endeavouring to mate.

The square outside looked quite deserted, with just the occasional passer-by.

Just then I heard the key turn in the door lock and Kay came in with my breakfast and although I had little appetite for food I did have a strong appetite to learn more about my situation.

Kay seemed to be quite friendly, if there was a strong sense of world-weariness about her. She lit a cigarette and said 'Well dear you have got yourself into a pretty unusual situation. The people you are now involved with are very dangerous – I am not supposed to know much other than that I have to look after your personal needs. But from what I have learned after being involved with Rahman – and also what I have overheard of late, your being here is very personal to him.

I asked her why she led a life working for such horrible people and she just pulled up her jumper to reveal a small bluebird tattoo on her wrist but above this her arms were pitted and blotched – My legs are in the same state deary, I have been a drug addict since leaving council care back in the 80s. That's how they operate. Pull in a girl with promises and then use a combination of the threat or actual use of violence and gradually get her hooked on drugs. A combination of fear and increasing dependency – the bastards.

Now, my worn body, beginning as a stripper, then porno films, then reduced to prostitution with a body left scarred after being sexually tumbled over by hundreds if not thousands of sweaty, often drunk, men.

They think that I am dependent on them, and that I am not too bright, so I am pretty much just a skivvy, serving drinks, running errands and from time to time looking after new girls like you. What they don't know is that my long-term fear and hatred of them all has changed to anger. But, so far, whenever I have resolved to break away my addiction kicks in. Kay's sadness was obvious in her heavy-lidded eyes, and I was already thinking that she might just be a possible link to my freedom.

I asked her to please explain more about why I am here if not to be forced into the vice industry.

She guided me towards the mirror – what do you see? I was unsure of what she meant and she went on to say that it is my Scandinavian looks, the long blond hair, the large clear blue eyes, the creamy pale skin, high cheek-bones and the general look.

'That is what Rahman wants' she said. 'And he wants it badly. He has no children of his own and he is the son of a man who emigrated to Britain from the Middle East and progressed from club bouncer to pimp, to running a string of girls and importing drugs. Building an extensive criminal organization during the 1970s,80s, and 90s. An organization that he then handed over to his eldest son Ashif.

I know all of this because unless they want something I am invisible to them, they hardly notice my presence and so I get to hear their gossip, much of which is bragging about their part in this or that activity. Rahman is given to repeating the story of his family and of how rich and powerful they have become. He has an office downstairs and for the past couple of months there has been an enlarged picture of you on the wall beside his desk. He is captivated by your looks, but not as a sexual companion, more as a brood mare.'

This picture was obviously the one taken by Lina when I had assumed that we were just enjoying each other's company in the Vilnius cafe.

Kay got up to leave, she said that she had said too much. Her final comment was to advise me to accept my new life as a birth mother to Rahman's babies. And to be relieved that he probably won't bother me for casual sex because she was sure that he is gay.'

John had been noting how Janina had become sadder as she unfolded her story and reaching out he put his hand on her shoulder and said

'That's enough now Janina, time to get some sleep.'

They both settled down for the night and in the few minutes before he drifted into sleep John thought back through the day. A day that began with him at Hunters Boatyard, tidying up his boat and letting the yard manager, Vickki, know that he had very reluctantly decided to sell his wooden half-decker. A boat, 'Curlew', that had given him so much pleasure in the last few years.

Just prior to preparing for bed John had e-mailed a Lowestoft based friend to ask if he could borrow his boat for a couple of weeks – they had sailed together a number of times and it was quite usual for the friend, Chris, to borrow John's Broads-based sailing boat and for John to borrow Chris's sea boat. A nicely convenient arrangement in that it allowed Chris to sail on the inland and only gently tidal Broads and for John to sail on the more challenging open sea.

What he did not know was that the two thugs encountered earlier in the day were now, just after midnight, heading towards Great Yarmouth, having had their bike fixed and their injuries treated. They had also been able to leave the police station with the police still considering whether or not to charge them for an uncorroborated assault on the receptionist. Following a wasted diversion tracking Janina's mobile phone to Cantly, they now assumed that their target's most likely destination was to have been Yarmouth.

One, now the pillion passenger, with his wrist in plaster, and both on strong pain killers. In addition to their physical injuries they were also nursing an intense hatred of the cause of their pain and a determination to do him serious harm.

They had phoned ahead to arrange to stay at a cheap hotel on the seafront and had already made contact with people they knew, or rather knew of, in the town.

These two thugs had come to Britain from their native Rumania where the police had been closing in and where, if caught, they faced long–term prison sentences for their involvement in a protection racket. A racket in which they were employed to frighten reluctant customers into compliance. On occasion, they had inflicted serious injury to the point that one victim had been killed and two others permanently disabled. The heavier thug, Mihai, now nursing a broken wrist, had realised how much he enjoyed inflicting pain even to the extent of feeling powerful during the gruesome process. Having criminal contacts in Britain, they were pushed from Romania due to police interest and pulled towards Britain by an awareness of the potential to make money from their antisocial talents.

Mihai, and his companion Florin, had both been members of the 'Noua Dreapta', a rag-bag group of socially dysfunctional individuals claiming to be heirs of the anti-Semitic, anti-communist, pro-fascist, 'Iron Guard'. An organization that had been politically active in Romania prior to and during the Second World War. And both of them had the Celtic Cross symbol of the group tattooed on their right bicep, as a complement to the Nazi symbol tattooed on their left bicep. The flesh between each containing the bodies of two men born into violent childhoods and being now shaped to view violence as a normal condition of social relationships.

Once in their hotel room these two were drinking pre-ordered vodka and eating sandwiches while they waited for the people they had ordered to meet them at the hotel as soon as possible. It wasn't long before three men dressed very casually were knocking gently on their door.

'Come in' called Mihai. These three were obviously quite nervous as they greeted the two visitors to their town.

'Right' said Mihai 'We are pissed that a woman on the run from us had been booked into a nearby hotel and that you pricks had not found her. Did you get the message sent previously to all locations where we have a presence? And the one sent earlier today that said we thought she was heading this way?'

The taller of the three men confirmed that they had received the messages but had been focusing a search on the town, making all of their street dealers aware of the emergency and issuing copies of the girl's picture that had been sent through.

'Christ man, we have been combing the town and resorts along the coast. But to be fair, we did not think it was likely that someone on the run would want to come to Norfolk, let alone Gt. Yarmouth.'

'You are not bloody paid to think.' Florin stood up and grabbing the man by the collar he pulled their faces together.

'She was tracked via her mobile phone to Acle and together they took a road off the Acle roundabout that leads directly to this town.'

Pulling out his phone he showed them a picture of the campervan.

'I have just sent this to you Danny – get this copied and distributed – we need to get these two bloody soon'.

Rees, the shorter of three men nervously asked

'Did you say couple? I thought we were only after a women.'

'Well now you are looking for a women and a man, some prick who took us by surprise and drove off with the women in a silver van.'

'Took you by surprise, was he armed?'

Now Mihai was clearly getting angry... 'No, he was not fucking armed but he tricked us and escaped, otherwise he would now be in the local accident and emergency unit struggling to stay alive. A place where you three might end up if you don't get straight fucking onto the search.'

Rees thought better than to comment on the bandaged wrist and obvious bruised looking Florin but it did seem odd that these two were injured and the guy had escaped.

'While we are on the subject of arms, I want two handguns and two spare magazines ideally 9mm Koch.... We don't carry them as a rule in case we get stopped by the police and we expect that local members of the Organization such as you can obtain firearms as and when required. He took a thick bundle of new £50 notes from his overnight bag and threw it onto the bed. That's our £10,000 artillery emergency fund and it should be enough to get a couple of handguns and some ammo in this poxy run-down town.'

As Rees, Danny, and Jimmy left the hotel Danny exclaimed. 'Fuck that, they were a couple of hard-looking bastards'

'Perhaps not as hard and the other guy' said Rees. 'And that's why that want fire-power'

'Christ Rees' said Danny. 'I thought that you had really upset them with the comment about their being surprised by this unknown guy. Anyway we are paid enough to take their shit and for us to do as we are told. They are only passing through. I am sure between us and our crew we can continue with the weekend's drug trading, as well as looking for this couple......Where would they go with a campervan? Jimmy, you organize a search of all the hotel and public car parks, and the 'Golden Mile' road along the seafront that could provide overnight parking. Rees you can go to the all-night garage on the southern edge of town and get copies made of the picture of the van and then we can get these out to the crew and seriously start combing the town.'

'If we do find them, I think we should leave it to those two foreign bastards to confront this guy,' said Jimmy

'So what about you Danny?'

'I will call into Russian Ted's gaff, I have already texted him from the hotel room to say I am on the way and am seeking two German toys'

'Why German toys?' queried Jimmy.

'Are you genetically stupid Jimmy 'German Toys' will mean German handguns to Ted. If I were to get arrested the first thing the filth would do would be to go through mobile phone messages – and OK, some drug deals would be on there, but we don't want them to read *'Can I have two Koch 9mm semi-automatic pistols and some ammo please Ted, pick up in an hour.'*

'Any evidence of gun use raises the stakes and would lengthen any jail sentence way beyond just dealing.'

Danny, Jimmy, and Rees, went their separate ways, Danny to collect the guns, Rees to get the photograph copied and Jimmy to start organising their local 'crew', or rather their local gang of drug peddlers and pimps working across Yarmouth and the towns running down the east coast.

All part of a tightly run network of drug dealers and brothel managers, with the drugs and girls provided by the country—wide network, with the 'Big Man' Rahman, at the top of the Organization. These three had graduated from shoplifting to burglary, and to the much more lucrative drug dealing, and were easily persuaded to join the London-based organization. It gave them a status with the local criminal classes and also protection, legal if necessary, and physical when required against criminal competition. A situation which gave these three very comfortable material lives and a nicely profitable criminal fiefdom to rule over.

At the campsite John woke early with a sense of unease. One caused by his remembering the photo taken as they left the hotel car-park in Acle the previous day. He was aware from personal experience – and his knowledge of targeted operations dealing with police corruption in which Metropolitan Police had been exposed – how easily criminals can infiltrate the police, and how straight-forward it would be to identify him, and then his police record, simply by using the van registration number and from this using the Met. data-base to access his police record, and so learn of his current circumstances. They might even be able to access the nationwide network of traffic management cameras to track the movement of the van. He was thinking that he had best assume that they could locate them fairly soon.

As a sailor John applied the navigational good practice that when endeavouring to identify the position of a boat at sea, using traditional navigation methods, your three-line plotting would mean that you invariably ended up with a small triangular area on a sea-chart within which your boat could be – given this scope for even a minor error, you would assume the corner of the triangle nearest any danger, submerged rocks, sandbanks, or wrecks, to be your position. A nautical interpretation of the precautionary principle. Consider the outcome of getting a decision wrong, and if this would be significant then minimise risk. It was this approach that he felt was required now......just assume they will turn up at the campsite fairly soon.

He woke Janina and told her that he thought they had best get moving.

'We will leave the van here, firstly because they are looking for it, and secondly because it might make them think that we are coming back to it. So allowing time for us to get away from this town. We can get cash in town, some spare clothes for you, and sufficient provisions to last a few days.'

'We won't need to get any cash John - look.....' With this, she lifted her handbag off the floor and pulled out a large bundle of cash – John let out a long whistle. 'Now that looks like thousands.'

'And that's not all' said Janina'

She then retrieved a smallish linen bag from the handbag and opening its pull-ties she emptied a stream of diamonds onto the table.

'Are they real? How on earth did you get these?' asked John.

'Well, these are linked to the next episode of the story of my imprisonment. But for now just call them a parting gift from Ashif Rahman.'

They hastily packed up the valuables, and some clothes John could find that he thought would be suitable, into his old rucksack. Before they left the van John sorted out a large woollen hat he used for sailing and suggested that Janina wear it so that most of her distinctive long blond hair could be hidden from view.

On their way John called into the reception office and, leaving his mobile phone number, he told the receptionist that he was expecting a couple of old friends to call in.

'So, if anyone comes to the reception to make inquires, can you please call me. But don't call until they have left the office as I want to surprise them.'

It was short bus-ride into the town, and they were soon walking along the windswept sea-front with its garish amusement arcades and themed fun-fare.

As it was still quite early in the day there were few people on the street and even fewer within the brave family groups endeavouring to find a spot that could offer at least some shelter from the north wind. A wind that was just strong enough for John to smile about as he considered his plan for the next stage of their journey. Not too strong, but sufficiently so for a decent sail, and blowing in the right direction for a passage across Breydon Water, the extensive stretch of tidal water running west from the town.

'We have all day to spend here Janina, so we best find somewhere even less busy if we can. Let's start with breakfast in that small cafe over there, it looks pretty empty. Then we can take stock of our situation.'

It did not take long for them to be served their scrambled eggs, fried bacon, toast, and mugs of strong tea by the cheerful cafe owner. Who asked if they were on holiday.

'No,' said John. 'We are just passing through on our way to Cromer.'

You never know thought John, if the thugs do trace us to here they could be put off the scent given that Cromer is on the north coast the opposite direction to the one I intend going.

'What's in those two plastic bottles?' asked Janina. 'Well' said John.

'These are a staple of the English diet. In one is what's called 'brown sauce', a concoction of all sorts of chopped up vegetables, molasses and vinegar, and other stuff you probably don't want to know about, the other is the even more popular 'tomato ketchup'. I would advise that you pass on both and just enjoy the food itself.'

'So, now we are truly on the run' said John. 'And given the money and more so the diamonds, in addition to Rahman's personal plans for you, I can understand why he is keen to track you, no us, down.'

'Can't we just go to the police?' said Janina.

'Well, I have thought about that but we are running from a significant criminal organization, based in London but with an intricate network spread across Britain.

I served as a police officer in London's Metropolitan Force for 1 years, I was fairly specialist in the Met's Specialist Firearm Unit SCO19, seconded to the Counter Terrorist Unit SO15. Even in the early 2000s I used to hear stories about possibly corrupt police officers. The scope for possible corruption in the Met. was initially revealed in the early 1980s with 'Operation Countryman'. An internal police investigation into certain activities by officers of the Met. Including members of the 'Flying Squad'...the infamous 'Sweeny Tod'. The findings were damning, 51 officers spread throughout the ranks, including three assistant commissioners, were identified, with possibly up to 250 other London-based police officers assessed to be involved in some form of corrupt activity, including colluding in the carrying out a series of crimes such as bank and payroll robberies. And in the Soho red-light district certain members of the Vice Squad were offering protection for vice-related businesses.

As recently as 2002, Operation Tiberius found that the Met. was so liable to corruption that organised criminals were even able to infiltrate New Scotland Yard itself' – 'New Scotland Yard?' queried Janina.

'Sorry' said John.

'That's the name of the building where the Met. has its Headquarters. I would like to think that the Met had cleaned up its act but given the power and reach of the organization that imprisoned you, I am not really confident enough to seek police protection. Would Rahman's power extend to the somewhat sleepy Norfolk constabulary...... well, who knows? But for the time being I think we should assume that it does......So, we are being sought by two thugs – plus possibly reinforcements sent from London – and we know that they have access to numerous drug dealers, pimps, and petty criminals in this region. Given this, I think that they will soon find the van, and hopefully they will assume that we will be returning to it so will stake it out for at least a day or so. Meanwhile we are going to try to steal a sailing boat from Gt Yarmouth Yacht Station and sail to Lowestoft from where we can exchange the inland Broads boat for my friend Chris's sea boat. We can then set off down the east coast. Opening distance from our chasers and allowing us time to think about how we manage the next stage – at some point I am thinking that we will have to confront this Rahman, either via the law or possibly more directly.'

'John, these are very dangerous men......From what I learnt from Kay and what I over-heard, they are killers, and they view a willingness to kill as a marker of their masculinity.'

'We are where we are Janina, and we can only deal with this situation as best we can, for now our lives have been drawn together, which is fine by me......and - as best we can - might surprise Rahman.'

Looking directly into her eyes he said.

'You have had a very stressful couple of days Janina, and this following a frightening period as a prisoner, so how do you feel?'

'My feeling are mixed...... yes I am very anxious, indeed still quite fearful, I think about my mumeda/mum and tevalis/dad back in Lithuania, not knowing what has happened to me, their only child. But I am also angry at the way I have been treated, and dearly wish to get back to my own country. I see Rahman as a source of such evil. Up until yesterday afternoon I was just running quite blindly, very scared and almost ready to give up, but meeting you has provided me with a source of emotional and physical strength that I can feel, and a sense that we might together actually win through. This does seem quite optimistic, but this is how I feel.'

'That's pretty positive Janina, so now we need to hide out in the town until nightfall and then make our way to the Yacht Station. There will I hope be some holiday boaters who will take advantage of being moored up in a larger town to seek out a restaurant for their evening meal. Leaving their boat for us to borrow.'

After lingering in the cafe for a couple of hours and four mugs of tea each, they made their way back out to the Marine Parade. John pointed to a low building across the main road.

'Look over there the 'Sea Life' aquarium, well that should keep us occupied for a while'.

They crossed over the wide road, paid the entrance fee, bought a colourful glossy-covered guidebook, and began their very slow examination of each marine-related exhibit.

Meanwhile, the hunters had been busy. Rees had arranged to have the picture of the van copied, and with Jimmy had organized handing them out to their contacts, individuals who were to some more or less extent linked to the criminal network. But by early afternoon no sightings had been reported.

Danny had made his way to the somewhat rundown part of the town within the dock area. An area that industrial development had passed by with only the ghosts lingering in the minds of some old Yarmouth men of the dozens of fishing trawlers that were now no longer off-loading their valuable catches at the port, and of the larger cargo boats that used to pass through the docks on their way down the wide River Yare and to the inland city of Norwich.

He parked his black, late model Porsche, in the car-park by the docks and walked into a narrow side street with a row of large terraced Edwardian houses. Once the impressive homes of sea captains and port officials, now primarily reduced to being houses of multiple occupation, each with numerous single or double rooms let at low-cost rent. Housing where the local council often placed the homeless that they had a statuary duty to house but whose numbers exceeded the town's available social housing stock.

In the middle of the terrace were four houses where the fronts had been extended and converted into small shops. In the row was a betting shop hosting illegal card schools in the backroom at weekends, a Kebab take-away, a massage parlour fronting for a brothel, and at the far end a shop selling air rifles and pistols, legal crossbows, cheap shotguns, and a range of ammunition and ancillaries to suit these.

The door of this last shop had a faded notice stating that it was only open Wed. Fri. and Sat. up to 4pm. As he entered the shop Danny took in the all-pervasive smell of the strong French Gauloise cigarettes chain-smoked by 'Russian Ted', the shop-owner and gunsmith.

'Christ, you just get uglier by the week Ted!'

'Yes, and you Danny get fucking richer no doubt' said Ted 'As you attempt to turn most of the young of Yarmouth and the other east coast towns into drug addled idiots.'

'Still Ted, at least this provides you with business as some of them pay you to convert the starting pistols and imitation guns they buy legally, or nick, into working handguns, used to steal goods or money to fund their habits'

'Well Danny, the Heckler and Koch working handguns you ordered are not easy to come by since the customs crackdown on weapons that had previously been easy to source from eastern European countries after the breakup of the Soviet Union. Back in the day we could get anything from a handgun to an automatic rifle or even ground-to-air missles.'

'Yea yea, go on Ted, you're just trying to talk up the price – let's see the goods.'

Ted had run his dubious business in the years since he had retired from long-term service as a private then sergeant armourer in 2 Para. A period of service that had seen two tours of duty in Northern Ireland and active service in the so called 'Falkland's War'. For him more a series of routs than hard battles as in a proper war. As poorly led, poorly equipped, and even more poorly trained Argentinean conscripts found themselves confronted by a well-trained, well-armed, and strongly motivated British Army. An army led by special force soldiers and the parachute regiment. To commemorate this last action, staged amongst the isolated chain of islands in the dreary, windswept and cold, south Atlantic, Ted had an Albatross in graceful gliding flight tattooed across his chest.

After turning the shop door sign over to indicate that the shop was closed, he led Danny down a steep set of stone steps, through a reinforced door, and into a large cellar. Although the air still smelt strongly of Gauloise this was now mingled with the smell of cordite and gun oil.

At one end of the room was a wide wooden bench with an old-fashioned vice attached to the side, and trays of gunsmith tools laid out along the back. In the front of which were two cantilevered desk lamps and a large magnifying glass set in a frame through which the detail of a gun's mechanism can be easily seen to work on.

Along one side of the long low-ceilinged cellar was a tunnel-like shooting range, its walls obviously thickly padded with sound proofing materials.

Ted moved a length of carpet aside and lifted a foot square section of a wide floorboard that was invisibly fitted in to the varnished wooden floor. He lifted out a folded sacking bag and set it out on the bench.

Removing two handguns and two boxes of ammunition.

'There you go......two new old stock – Heckler and Koch 9mm semi-automatic compact handguns and four ammunition clips of 15 rounds each. Yours for 20K'

Danny picked up one of the guns and as he felt its comforting weight he immediate felt powerful, bigger than he was, such is the affect that a gun can have on the weak-minded.

Ted could see the subtle change in Danny's demeanour.

'Yes, these babies will deter pretty much any of the opposition that you are liable come across in Britain, and cheap at the price.'

'Ted, I have ten grand and I want both guns, so you will need to drop on the daft price you mentioned.'

Ted's pause before responding suggested a reluctance to accept Danny's offer.

'Look Ted, I am buying these for two guys up from our base in London and I think that you know what that means if you upset them. We have always had a good working relationship so let's cut the crap. I suspect that ten grand would still give you at least a 100% profit. But if I meet up with the London guys with just one gun then they might well be back here tomorrow themselves, and they will then be armed.'

Ted puffed out his florid cheeks......'OK, yea, I can manage with ten, let's face it I won't be paying tax!'

Leaving the shop with the sack containing the guns now in a Tesco's plastic shopping bag, he drove back to the hotel. On the way he called Rees and Jimmy to check on progress with the hunt.

'No definite sighting yet Danny' said Rees 'But just now we were cruising along the sea-front and we could see a couple of campervans and one of them motorhomes parked up at the far end of Marine Parade. We stopped and showed a picture of the van we are looking for around and one old fella said that, although they had not seen such a van, he asked if we had checked out the official campsite sited by the horse-racing track on the outskirts of town.'

'Fuck me!' interrupted Danny. 'Why the fuck did we not think of that – the times we have been to weekend race meetings – what a bunch of pricks we are!'

'Yes, and that's probably what the guys back at the hotel will think' piped up Jimmy.

'Now, you two get along to the campsite and I will get to the hotel. If the van is there call me straight away and I will try to manage our London friends.'

'We are already on our way,' said Rees.

When he got back to the hotel Danny found the two thugs smoking dope and watching the movie 'Pulp Fiction' on a laptop.

'I love this film, nicely casual violence, what do you think Danny.'?

'Yes, all good, I like the ending best.'

He opened his bag and took out the guns. Florin and Mihai handled, no more caressed, one each and with an obviously well practiced movement quickly inserted a magazine and both swung their weapons up to point at Danny's head.

'For Christ sake' said Danny

'Just joshing Danny, nice guns, good job.'

'Mr unknown fuck-pig is going to have at least two 9mm slugs in his guts before too long.'

Danny's 'We are the Champions' ring tone alerted him to a call he had been waiting for.

'Danny the van's here' said an excited Rees. Florin having overheard snatched the phone from Danny.

'Are our targets with the van?'

'No' said Rees.

'But we have been to the campsite reception and the bird there told us that they had left earlier today and had said they should be back later on. What do you want us to do?'

'Pull back, and keep well out of sight, we will be there late this afternoon......But of course, if they do come back early then call us immediately, do not try to contain them, clear?'

'Yes, that's fine' said Rees, thinking that in any case he would prefer not to have to tackle this guy with just the two of them. He was thinking that even the baseball bat (his 'persuader') that he kept in the boot of his car might not tip the balance. If this guy could deal with the tough London pair then he must be quite a handful.

The time John and Janina spent in the aquarium was an interlude of almost other worldliness as they immersed themselves in the creatures of the underwater world and their various types of habitats. The large tanks of multicoloured fish darting this way and that way amongst the modelled coral reefs, with others keeping close to the rocky ledges on which grew seaweeds and on which lived bright anemones and under which the large grey head of a moray eel could be seen ...the larger fish, rays, and sharks, drifted easily around the large tank.

Then they noticed an octopus as it, almost seeming to flow, moved along the bottom of the tank as if following the pair.

John pointed to the creature.

'I have recently read a book that suggests octopuses have a type of conscious awareness far more developed than had previously been assumed. They have been on earth for possibly as long as 290 million years, so back to the time when dinosaurs were the dominant land creatures. Apparently, they can even be taught to navigate their way through simple mazes, and researchers studying these generally shy creatures say that they seem to learn to recognise the humans they encounter – and to obviously track their movements.'

'astonājis'! said Janina then in response to John's quizzical look said

'astonājis is Lithuanian for octopus' she explained.

'Such odd creatures' 'Yes,' observed John.

'But then as you can see all around us just now, much of the undersea world is populated with exotic creatures.'

Following a light sandwich lunch in the aquarium cafe, they made their way into the town centre.

'I have one more place to visit on this relatively brief tour of the town Janina' said John.

'And I think the fishy theme will continue. It's three o'clock and we do have a couple more hours to fill before we can go to the Yacht Station.'

The sky was overcast now, and John could sense rain on its way. But as long as the breeze continued quite strong and blowing from the north, he was happy.

They crossed back over Marine Parade and walked towards the town centre. On a narrow street running directly from the seafront they came across the 'Fishing Museum' that John had remembered seeing when previously in the town.

As they approached the entrance John's phone went off. It was the receptionist at the campsite. 'Hi' John answered the call. 'It looks like your friends have arrived' said the receptionist

'And I am just letting you know as you asked me to.'

'Yes, thanks June (he had remembered the name on her jacket badge) ......What did you tell them?'

'Only that you were out for the day and due to come back later in the evening.'

'That's brilliant, thanks very much, I expect we will see them soon.'

As he ended the call John thought that now hopefully the opposition will be focused on the van, anticipating their return that evening. He was somewhat relieved to think that they now had a breathing space, easing some of the more immediate pressure. But then, thinking of the reach of the mob they were facing, he suspected that they might still have people looking out for them in the town.

The fishing museum, that they could see was actually named 'Time and Tide', was located in a substantial red-brick Victorian building with large iron gates leading to the side entrance. A sign painted along the brickwork above the ground floor windows read JNR TOWER CURING WORKS 1880, indicting a previous life where the primary activity had been the smoking of the fish caught in the sea off the east coast.

Having paid the entrance fee they walked slowly round the museum, each with earphones through which they could listen to a running commentary of the history of the building and of the related fishing industry based in Great Yarmouth. Just as they were setting off John turned to Janina and whispered.

'Another learning opportunity Janina to follow the aquarium, and I will be testing your knowledge after our visit.'

'Oh yes, and I will probably have taken in more information than you.' she joked. It was good for John to see that she is smiling at last after what she has been through.

What they did learn was that Gt Yarmouth had been involved in the fishing industry going back to the time of the 'Doomsday Book' in 1085 CE, when the activity was first recorded. An industry based on catching and processing (mainly by the preservative technique of 'smoking') the herring fish.

An industry that grew steadily in terms of the amount of fish landed up to its most prosperous period in the early 20th century, when there were as many as 700 Scottish fishing boats working out of the port throughout the herring season. A time when the whole of the wide harbour would be packed with steam-driven drifters landing hundreds of tons of the shiny, nutritious, fish each week. A harvest of the sea to be processed by hundreds of 'fisher girls', often the wives and daughters of the fishermen. All together working their way down the east coast of Britain from their homes in Scotland, as they followed the steady southward migration of the vast shoals of herring. A record year being 1913 when 12 million tons of herring were landed.

Such relentless fishing was a primary factor in the gradual decline of the industry until, by the 1950s, the Scot's boats had ceased to come south and herring fishing in Yarmouth was reduced to just a few small inshore fishing boats landing quite modest catches.

In addition to learning some history of herring fishing, the pair also took in the range of exhibits illustrating the living conditions of lower paid workers during the Victorian and Edwardian times, as well as some of the tin and wooden toys and the story books that helped to fill the time and stimulate the imagination of children.

As they left the museum John asked Janina what she had learned about the fishing industry – 'Well, apart from obviously being an important part of the history of this seaside town, the demise of the herring seems to reflect the extent of the way we have more generally over-exploited the bounty of the sea – to the point where fish stocks are in a parlous state. We have a similar situation in Lithuania and the other Baltic states, with declining fish stocks in fisheries dependant on the harvest of the Baltic Sea'

'Yes, what with the aquarium and its various marine conservation programs and the over-fishing noted here, we have had a quite shocking 'heads-up' on the impact of humankind on the beautiful and bounteous oceans.'

They walked on in reflective silence as a light drizzle began to fall from a grey-clouded sky.

Making their way further into the town John directed Janina into a clothes shop.

'Right, we need to buy some gear for the next few weeks, especially warm underwear.'

It didn't take too long for them to emerge back into the street with a couple of bags containing his and her underwear, four shirts, two thickly knitted polo necked jumpers and a light waterproof suit each. Then it was into the small supermarket next door to buy what John estimated would be sufficient basic toiletries and foodstuffs – milk, bread, coffee, tea bags, baked beans, sardines, butter, bananas, apples, water biscuits and various types of chocolate bars - to last for at least a few days until they could replenish their stocks.

It was early evening by the time they arrived at the Yacht Station situated on the eastern bank of the River Bure just before it completed its meandering journey from deep within the Norfolk countryside to join the North Sea here in Yarmouth.

The Yacht Station was composed of a fairly modern, single storied brick-built Broads Authority office, with a long stretch of mooring on the eastern bank of the river. Along which an assortment of sailing and motorboats were moored up for an overnight stay. They would be setting off tomorrow, some heading north to explore the extensive northern Broads and for others it would be south across Breydon and into the southern river network. And it was the Breydon route and then the River Waveney and across Oulton Broad to the port of Lowestoft that John was intending to use as an escape route.

In a quiet road just back from the river they found a rundown pub that was 'open all day'. The pub was empty apart from a bored looking girl behind the counter and a couple of old boys sitting in a corner of the large bar playing cribbage. They looked up and briefly acknowledged the newcomers before bending straight back to their game. John bought the coke that Janina wanted and a half-pint of bitter for himself. Having settled at a table from where they could take in most of the road, John told Janina that he was going to take a walk over to the moorings just to see if he could identify a boat that would suit them.

'You stay here – the moorings are quite exposed, and they would be looking of a couple so I should pass unnoticed. I'll only be ten to fifteen minutes.'

As he walked along the mooring area he could identify a couple of the 'Hunters' traditional 'for hire' sailing boats that he had been hoping would be here. Boats that he knew pretty well. The first one, with its name 'Hustler 2' painted in blue and red script on its transom, had the canvas cockpit cover on and it was obvious that the occupants were not on board. But about a hundred yards further on two couples were standing on the paved bank beside the other 'Hunters' boat 'Lucent' chatting together. Walking past he sat down on a seat by the office within hearing distance of the small group.

He noticed that they were engaged in quite a bit of small talk, but also that two of the four had hand-luggage type bags on the ground next to them. The small talk went on for about five minutes before the younger of the two men said 'OK then, we will be here until quite late tomorrow morning so we will keep an eye on your boat. What hotel will you be stopping at. The other male replied that it would be the 'Imperial Hotel' and the women standing next to him said.

'Yes, it will be good to get some decent food, a properly warm shower, and a night's sleep in a soft bed after a week on the pretty basic Hunters boat.'

This was just what John was hoping to hear. He had expected that there might be a suitable boat which was unoccupied due to the holiday sailors going in the town for an evening meal, but to learn that one boat would be left unoccupied overnight was ideal.

He was soon back at the pub setting out his plan to Janina.

'It will be dark in an hour or so and we can slip aboard the yacht I have identified and set off. It is illegal to sail at night without navigation lights, but the Board Authority Police patrol boats are not usually on the water after dark.'

After another drink each and a shared packet of salted peanuts they left the pub which had been slowly filling up with a motley collection of what seemed to be regulars. John did briefly hold eye contact with a stylishly dressed youngster leaning on the bar, whose youth and assertively smart demeana made him stand out.

They crossed the road, and cautiously made their way along the moorings to 'Lucent', where John slipped on board and eased open the small padlock on the cabin door. Before they left the pub John had checked the tide times on his phone and was able to inform his new 'crew' that.

'The water was now between tides so 'slack', which will allow the natural flow of the river to take us gently along. If you take the tiller I will cast off.'

'But I have never sailed,' said Janina.

'Don't worry, we won't have the sails up yet so steering will be easy as we just drift down river. As we leave the mooring just push the tiller gently away from your body'. And then I will tell you which way to move it.'

John untied the mooring rope (a 'warp' in sailing parlance) at each end of the boat and firmly pushed her off, stepping deftly on board as she moved toward the middle of the river.

'That's great' said John.

'Now just straighten the tiller and hold her there whilst I clear the decks ready to lower the mast.'

'Why lower the mast....I thought that we would be sailing?'

'We sure will in this lovely breeze once we get under the A47 road bridge between us and the open water of Breydon and to do this we need to lower the mast. But before we can progress we will have to wait in the basin between here at the bridge for at least an hour before the new inflowing tide is strong enough to take us under the bridge.

'Why not just start the engine and motor under?' asked Janina.

John smiled broadly.

'Well that is sort of the point of retaining these old boats as original, no engines, just sailing skills'

Within about 15 minutes they were turning past the large yellow navigation post marking the end of the River Bure and had moved into the basin. From where the silhouetted outline of the road bridge could just be made out.

'So we have to anchor here?' said Janina, feeling pleased that she had made a nautical reference.

'Well, not exactly, we will be 'mud weighting', no anchor on these boats. Just a heavy weight on the end of a length of rope that sticks in the soft mud lining the bed of the Broads rivers and lakes, anchors would just slip through this type of mud.' He explained.

John moved forward and dropped what look to be a substantial round lump of metal tied to a longish length of rope over the side. The boat slowed to a stop as the slack between the boat and the sinking weight was soon taken up and she came to a halt. Just shifting slightly from side to side in the much reduced flow.

Coming back to the open cockpit area behind the cabin where Janina was sitting, John sorted out the cooking equipment, found a box of matches in a draw, and soon had a kettle heating on one of the paraffin powered cooking rings. He also lit two of the brass oil lamps fitted into gimballed lamp-holders attached to the cabin sides. He then pulled a warm coat from his rucksack and another from the shopping bag from the town shop. Handing one to Janina he said.

'It's beginning to get a lot cooler now so put this on. I am hoping that the wind will keep up for at least long enough for us to sail across Breydon. For now, we are here for at another hour or so, so let's pick up on your story of escape.'

They settled with tea and hastily made cheese sandwiches and, as Janina finished a mouthful of sandwich, she gathered her thoughts and continued her story.

'In the hotel my life became a pattern of eating, Koranic studies, online shopping, and gaming, and each afternoon my being allowed a longish walk accompanied by Florin or another of the thugs. I did ask for some books and Kay bought me a bundle of paperbacks all published by a 'Mills and Boon' – Each one setting out a sickly story of idealised romance with cardboard characters living lives of minor dramas being escalated into crises, and with these being resolved, so each book ending with an happy couple walking off into the sunset arm-in-arm. I soon got bored with these and asked if I could have some more interesting reading material.

They did relent and with two thugs, Frank and Lewis, I was taken along to Housmans Bookshop not far from the Square. It reminded me so much of the cosy bookshop in Vilnius and the enjoyment I found in working there – up to but a month or so previously.

I think my guards, or rather the thugs, missed the theme of the shop which even as a foreigner I could see was quite politically left wing. The shelves were lined with a range of Marxist, socialist, and even anarchist books.

Whilst looking at the piles of books an obviously bored Lewis held up a 2000 page, three volume, book titled 'The Human Condition' by an author named Ernest Dyer – Lewis's assessment was along the lines of 'Fuck me what kind of dick would write this crap? Still, I suppose given its size we could use it to hold a door open. But at £60 a poke it's a bloody expensive lump.' I mention this John so that you can see the sort of cretins that we are dealing with.

I did not get 'The Human Condition', thinking it was probably too much of a challenge even for me. But I did ask for a copy of a much shorter book by the same author with the intriguing tile of 'On Being Human' – the title alone suggesting that it should be something to be read by Frank, Lewis, and their friends, so that they might have learned what it means to be human in a good way rather than in their cruel way. With this book, a couple of history books, and four novels we made our way back to the hotel.

In the month that I was held in the hotel I was twice taken along to Rahman's office on the ground floor. The first time he was already there sitting behind his desk examining some diamonds – he held up a large one of these to the light and asked me if I would like to have it mounted in a gold ring as the first wedding gift. I would admit that after what Kay had told me about this man I was quite frightened, but a part of me was angry and trying to formulate a plan of escape. So I just asked if I could have my freedom instead.

He just smiled, 'Good to see that you have retained a sense of humour my dear.' I shuddered at this term of affection, but I also noticed that he put the small bag of diamonds in the central draw of his desk and I caught a glimpse of a bundle of banknotes on top of a well-thumbed hardback notebook. This notebook...'she said as she drew it from her bag.

'What more are you going to pull from the magic bag Janina.... diamonds, money, and now a notebook......Let's have a look through it while you carry on,' said John.

'About a week later I was again taken by Frank down to the office but this time Rahman wasn't there. Frank indicated a settee and told me to wait until Rahman came. He then left the room. This gave me a chance to try the draw which I found slid open quite easily. I had just managed to close it and walk back to the settee when Rahman came lumbering into the office. As previously, he asked me to stand up and turn around but at least on these visits I was allowed to keep my clothes on. He sat beside me of the sofa and, taking my hand into his huge sweaty paw, he told me that I would be a having a medical examination the next day and that the 'virgin reversal' operation would be undertaken a week later in a place he called Harley Street. Which seemed an odd place to have an operation rather than a hospital. But of more concern to me was the intended assault that was to take place on my body.....not just the physical operation but an attempt to, in effect, erase part of my past. It probably seems silly but although I was long over the relationship with the boy I had met at university, losing my virginity was a bitter-sweet moment in my very person biography.

I left the office determined to escape if I could before the operation.'

John held up his hand...'Hold on Janina, I have only been able to glance through this notebook, but it seems to be an account of payments made to a number of quite senior police officers, and a couple of politicians that I have heard of – names, amounts, and dates when payments were made. There are also lists of what seem to be the regional level operatives in their drug trade network.

This could be dynamite in terms of exposing this bunch of crooks.'

'But for now, go on with your story Janina'

'So, during the week since that last visit to the office I had to undergo a detailed and intrusive medical examination by a heavy-handed woman doctor who refused to give me her name. But I also had a chance to talk with Kay who told me more about the extent of Rahman's empire. It was as if he was some horrible black spider sitting at the centre of web spread throughout Britain, with anyone getting caught in it having to suffer as he fed on their weakness or fear. Such is the drug and prostitution based empire he controlled.

Kay was obviously embittered by the way in which she was being treated as a skivvy for the gang. She told me that she was once a real 'queen' when she was Rahman's younger brother's girl. This brother seemed to get a kick out of watching Kay perform with other men and sometimes girls in porno films. That was the time that she said that she really got hooked on cocaine. Up to then she was able to manage it more as a recreational drug. I remember the sad look in her teary eyes when she said that '.... it gradually seeps into your mind until it controls you.'

She was still quite distressed when she got up to leave and as I moved to the door with my arm around her painfully thin shoulders I asked her if she could just leave the door unlocked so that I could wash and dry some underwear in the laundry room. I told her not to worry because I had resigned myself to my fate, at least for now. And that as she would be the first person here in the morning no one would know that she had helped me. I held my breath as I waited for Kay's answer. 'You know', she said 'This would be a tiny act of rebellion against their stupid controlling rules, so bugger them.' But then she said that even if I did try to leave the hotel there were guards posted downstairs 24 hours a day...... mainly to ensure the smooth running of the shady sex-based business of the hotel but also tasked with making sure that Janina doesn't leave.

Learning this was obviously a set-back, but I was determined to at least try to escape. If the memory of Florin's comment on my first day of imprisonment about what would happen if I did not cooperate did cause a moment of doubt. The thought of being, in effect, owned by Rahman and to give birth to children that he would surely bring up to follow in his evil foot-steps, made up my mind to go for it.'

Janina was clearly becoming tired.

'It's been long day' said John.

'And I can tell from the movement of the boat that the tide is now starting to flow in from the sea, so we best get moving – lets pause the story for now with you on the point of escape and we can continue tomorrow.'

John went forward to lift the mud-weight and as it came free of the muddy riverbed the boat moved slowly forward. He came back to the cockpit and took control of the tiller. Soon the dark angular shape of the A47 road bridge passed above them and the lights from the occasional traffic using the bridge were reflected from the surface of the water.

John steered the boat to the floating mooring platform specifically placed for boats to tie up whilst they raised their masts and prepared to set off down Breydon. He moored head to wind to ease the sail raising operation and it did not take him long to raise the mast, this due mainly to its nicely balanced lead counterweight offsetting the weight of the solid wooden mast.

Once the mast was secured the next step was to firstly tie on and raise the jib sail and then, by hand over hand, to raise the heavy gaff to which the mainsail was attached. The operation went well. Due primarily, John reflected, to the first-class maintenance of these Hunters boat.

Initially the two sails of the gaff-rigged boat flapped quite gently in the breeze, but once he had released the mooring rope and eased the boat off the wind, the sails began to fill and as he took up the slack in the main and jib sheets, so hardening the sails, the boat soon gained speed until they were cruising along creating a white-foamed bow wave as they pressed on into the night-dark surface of a wind whipped Breydon.

This was always a magical moment for John. Casting off for a sail and ensuring that the sails were well set in order to make efficient progress in a decent breeze was such a life enhancing feeling – 'just the best' he thought, but he then reflected on the situation they were in.

Janina had fallen asleep on one of the bunks in the main cabin and she looked so peaceful in contrast to the turbulent few weeks she had just experienced.

John's hand tightened on the tiller, but he was wishing that it could be holding the flabby neck of this Ashif Rahman who was responsible for their having to run.

Pulling up the collar of his coat John sailed into the darkness of Breydon. He could just about make out the navigation posts lining each side of the deep main channel passing through the wide expanse of water. Red posts on the port (left) side and green posts on the starboard (right) side. If for him these were just darkened shapes guiding his passage.

As 'Lucent' was pushing on across Breydon a hundred miles south what looked like a bundle of old clothes was drifting slowly down the River Thames. At the point down river at Woolwich where the free ferry criss-crossed the river each day during daylight hours this bundle brushed alongside the tall black hull of a moored ferry boat. A pale-skinned lifeless human hand with a small, faded, bluebird tattoo on the inner wrist could be seen extending from it. The bundle contained the body of Kay – She had paid the price of being held even just partly responsible for Janina's escape. Each of the guards at the hotel had only received a beating, Kay was more easily dispensable, indeed disposable.

Chapter Two

It was about 3 am when John steered 'Lucent' deep into the reed-bed where Breydon ended and the River Waveney began. After tying her up and lowering the sails, he laid down on the cabin bed opposite Janina and slept until the Sun came up a couple of hours later. He woke to the smell of frying eggs and was soon sitting next to Janina in the cockpit enjoying eggs and buttered bread with their first mug of coffee.

'What a nice day,' said Janina.

'And the reeds look so lovely swaying in the breeze.'

As they looked over the extensive reed-bed they could see a pair of large broad-winged birds cruising slowly overhead.

'Marsh Harriers' said John.

'These were once quite rare birds on the Broads, but they have been making a comeback in recent years, benefiting from farmers reducing the spraying of pesticides, and with gamekeepers deterred by recently introduced laws to continue the practice of putting poisoned baits down intending to kill the Harriers whose pray included some of the chicks reared for the tweed coated leisure shooters/huntsmen to blast out of the sky.

'They are so graceful as they fly around' observed Janina.

'What they are doing now is called 'quartering,' said John. 'As they slowly fly in ever moving circles across the reed-bed looking for even the tiniest of movements amongst the reeds that might indicate some water vole, small bird, or similar meal.'

In the daylight Janina could now get a better look at the boat.

'If the birds are graceful then this boat is beautiful, all the varnished wood and clean brass fittings. How old is it John?'

'Unusually, this particular boat 'Lucent' was only built just last year. Whereas the rest of the boats in the Hunters fleet were made between the 1930s and the 1950s. 'Lucent' was something of an experiment to see if they could now make a boat of the same design as the older boats and do this without a proper 'plan', as the originals had been lost.

The chief boat-builder at Hunters was Graham the foreman, who had spent most of his working life helping to maintain the Hunters fleet of thirteen 28ft/30ft sailing cabin cruisers, similar to Lucent, and seven half-deckers. These lovely boats have hulls made of mahogany. And, as I mentioned earlier, they are kept in the same state – no engines, no electrics – just as when they were first constructed.

I think I also mentioned that my own boat 'Curlew' is moored at Hunters so I was able to follow 'Lucent' gradually taking shape when the boat was being built at the yard. A project led by Graham, progressively and skilfully transforming a massive log of mahogany into the beautiful boat we are now sitting in. Traditional skills made obvious at the end of each summer when the boats are lifted from the water and stored in cradles in the two large wooden boat sheds that overlook a reed lined Hunters Dyke linked to the longer 'Fleet Dyke' and from there out into the wide River Thurne.

Once the boats were safely in the shed the men begin their well practised winter routine of repair and more general maintenance. All in order to prepare the fleet for the next season's batch of holiday hirers.

To enter the shed in the winter Janina is to step back into the 1930s. The bare hulls of the boats, the masts neatly stacked on elongated shelving, the canvas sails hanging up to air, the brightly varnished wooden blocks through which the sail-sheets run, and masses of rigging and other ropes, all carefully packed away. The sheds are pervaded with the smell of paint, linseed oil, of varnish, anti-foul, and of old wooden boats slowly drying out.'

She could see that John was seeing the boats in his imagination and reaching out she gently placed her hand on his shoulder.

'You obviously love these old boats John.'

'Yes, in a modest way it is a privilege to be able to share the Hunters experience and indeed to be able to keep 'Curlew' there.'

As he was saying this he was mentally beginning to question his intention to sell 'Curlew'.

By 9 o'clock they had cleared away the breakfast dishes and were preparing to set sail while back at the seafront hotel their chasers were meeting up in the hotel lounge, after having pointedly informed the manager that the lounge was temporarily closed to other guests.

Now scattered on armchairs around the shabby lounge were Danny, Rees, Jimmy, and four of their local gang members. Rees and Jimmy and been relieved of their stake-out task in the early hours by two other local villains.

On one wall of the lounge a large flat-screen TV was on but with the sound off.

A now quite dishevelled and obviously angry Florin and Mihai stood in front of Danny, Rees, Jimmy and the four local gang members.

'So, the bastards did not turn up at the van last night. I expect they must have seen you two dicks and you were probably heads down playing stupid games on your phones when they walked past.'

'No, Florin' said Rees.

'We took turns to stay alert, honest.'

'Well whatever happened' snapped Mihai. 'They seem to have fucking disappeared.'

Just then a smartly dressed member of the gang jumped up from his chair rushed over to the T.V. and turned the sound up.

'Look the Yacht Station, they just flashed up a 'stolen boat' story.' On the screen a reporter from the local T.V.

station 'Look East' was standing on the quay at the yacht station interviewing the couple that had taken to a comfortable hotel rather than stop on 'Lucent' the previous evening.

'Yes,' said the man. 'When we arrived back here this morning we found the boat gone and we immediately called the police!'

The Broads Authority officer who had been standing in the background confirmed that they had security camera footage of the boat leaving the mooring about 9 pm last night.

'What the fuck are you playing at with the TV said Florin'

'Well, I had arrived to organize some deals in the pub across the road from the river moorings early yesterday evening and I saw a couple leaving the pub that could have been the two we are looking for.'

Florin advanced menacingly toward the speaker and pointed his index finger straight into his face.

'Well why the fuck didn't you raise the alarm last night you dickhead.'

'I wasn't sure, I knew you had the van staked out and had been expecting that they would be returning to it and my sighting was so brief I did not want to make a prick of myself'

'Too fucking bad, as that is just at you have done, in spades!'

'Hold on, I can understand why you are upset Florin' said Danny.

'But let's not waste time arguing about what we might or might not have done, let's think about what we do now'.

Oh, so you're the fucking brains now Danny' said Florin.

Mihai stepped forward. 'Just calm down Florin, Danny's right. Let's focus on where they would have gone in the boat. Surely it can't be far, would they have gone out to sea?'

'Unlikely' said Rees. 'My dad had one of these Broads boats they have what's called a low freeboard and a small keel, so can only really manage on the shallower, calmer, inland waters. They must have sailed across Breydon. The issue would be that when they had made the crossing they would have the choice of taking the River Yare to Norwich or the River Waveney down to Beccles or some village or town along the way.'

'I guess Norwich seems the most obvious' said Danny.

'From there they can catch a train or coach to pretty much anywhere. Do we have a map?'

In just a few minutes Jimmy was back with a map of the Broads supplied by the hotel manager. Spreading it out on a table they could see Breydon Water and the two rivers running into its southern end. As they were taking in the detail Mihai pointed to a coastal town, with some docks that seemed, like Yarmouth, to be linked to an inland lake/Broad. If one nowhere near as big as Breydon.

'Where is that?' he asked.'

'Lowestoft' said Rees 'And the inland lake is called Oulton Broad and the stretch of open water from the road bridge to the sea is Lake Lothing. It's a fair sized town from which they could take a train south'.

'Or steal another boat from the marinas marked as being in the town itself.' Suggested Mihai

'This time presumably a sea-going boat......so their next stop could be Norwich, Beccles, or perhaps Lowestoft.'

'Right then, you Rees and Jimmy, take a couple of your mates and get to Norwich, you Florin go with the other two down to Beccles, and Danny and I will take the bike down to Lowestoft. Then we have two armed pairs and there will be four of you. If you have to, then take the guy on in Norwich. This dick is dispensable so use lethal force if necessary.'

As these went their separate ways Lucent was sailing south along the Waveney. 'What on earth is that big sailing boat?' asked Janina as she pointed to a 60ft long craft with a mast the size a thickish tree-trunk from which an expanse of black canvas sail billowed in the wind.

'That is a Wherry' said John 'Up to early in the 19th century there used to be hundreds of them working on the Broads, they were the cargo carrying work-horse and whole families often lived aboard. The coming of the railways and increasing road transport led to the gradual demise of those boats and many of them were just burnt or sunk to serve as barriers to protect reed-beds from the eroding wash of passing boats.

I think there are now about half-dozen left, being used to take tourists on day trips. They are still maintained by the same sort of traditional boat-builders that work at Hunters. But on a bigger scale with the Werrys.'

'I feel that I am learning so much about this area you call the Broads, the boats, the wildlife, and some of the people.'

'And I think that when we get to sea you are going to learn much more about sailing.'

John was thinking ahead and hoping that his friend Chris's boat 'Sunrise' was prepared for a sail, with the fuel and fresh water tanks full, and at least some food on board.

As the morning drew on the wind picked up and by lunch-time they were leaving the River Waveney and had sailed into the narrow Oulton Dyke leading down to Oulton Broad. It only took half an hour for them to sail across the small Broad and moor alongside the Wherry Hotel at the eastern side of the Broad.

'Now we have got to move fast' said John 'We have to assume that they could be close.'

His assumption was justified, and even as they were tying the mooring ropes Mihai and Danny were standing in the shadow of the Hotel watching them. They had sped down from Yarmouth, with Danny driving the powerful Kawasaki 750cc motor-bike with a style of driving bordering on reckless. Mihai's wrist was still sore but the plaster-cast fitted at the hospital held it in place and the primary symptom was being suppressed with strong pain-killers, at least sufficiently for him to have the confidence that he could still pull the trigger on the Koch as soon as they had an opportunity. They just required a more secluded location, if one with sufficient background noise to mask the sound of the shot.

John and Janina packed their bags with clothes, toiletries, and what food they had left and quickly made their way across the main road, then they ran along the narrow pathway on the southern side of Lake Lothing coming to the impressive white building of the 'Royal Norfolk and Suffolk Yacht Club' looking out to its club Marina and to the north sea beyond the grey stone harbour wall. It was here John knew that Chris moored his yacht. As it is standard practice for any sailing club to allow non-members sailors to their amenities, John felt that they could take advantage of this traditional hospitality and use the club-house showers before they set off.

John tapped gently on the club secretary's office door and on entering found a jovial looking white haired and white bearded man sitting behind a desk. The walls of the small room were lined with a range of pictures of men, and a few women, standing proudly on the decks of a variety of types of boat. There was also a glass-fronted and varnished wooden cabinet showing off some highly polished silver sailing cups standing on a silky blue material base.

'Hi' said John 'We have arranged to borrow Chris Vardy's boat, he was going to let you know'.

'Ah yes' said the club secretary 'Chris e.mailed me this morning so all good as far as we are concerned'

'I will write down the code of the Marina security gates for you, we change this each month.'

While he was doing this John noticed through the net curtains a couple of men standing outside, one leaning casually against the wire fence of the Marina the other with a plaster on his wrist, looking towards the club house door.

John immediately recognised Mihai from the Acle Hotel. Well, there still only seems to be two of them but this time I won't have the element of surprise. They seem to be waiting for us so I think we will let them stew while we shower.'

John had not allowed for Mihai's strong urge to confront him as soon as possible – his need for revenge was heighten by having seen John again.

John and Janina made their way to the male and female showers. Following a quick shower John had dried himself and was just strapping his watch back on when the door of the men's shower room burst open.

Mihai and Danny had entered the club house and had left the secretary lying badly injured on the office floor, his blood trickling across the beige carpet. When these two had walked straight into his office without knocking he had taken an instant dislike to them and had refused to answer the abrupt question about the couple that were using the showers. A refusal that had seen Danny walk round the desk and pull the secretary out of the chair by his hair. Then Mihai pulled the pistol and hit the man hard on the back of his head.

'Stupid bastard.......I so hate these posh gits' said Danny dropping the body onto the floor.

Now they were confronting John with just a towel round his waist. A wide grin lit up Mihai's face.

'Now we have you, you bastard, he raised the gun and as he did so Janina, having heard the exchange, threw the door open, knocking Danny to one side. The second that Mihai's focus left John as he turned very slightly towards the door John leapt forward, brushing the gun aside as it fired, and aiming a powerful kick to Mihai's genitals.

He went down as if poll-axed, and the gun clattered across the tiled floor. Danny came gingerly forward but his right hand punch lacked much in the way of conviction and John just moved into the swinging arm and hit Danny squarely in the solar plexus. The wind went out of him as did his consciousness when John followed up with a fierce left hand uppercut. Turning to Mahai, he saw him crawling towards the gun but Janina stepped forward and stamped down hard on his plastered wrist. Now Mihai was in serious trouble and John's kick to the side of his head sent him into a similar state of unconsciousness as was Danny.

Picking up the gun, John could see that it still held about 14 bullets. He then realised that in the fight he had lost the towel and he stood exposed. 'Hm....not too bad a physique for an old man' said Janina as she handed him his trousers.

Before they left the sailing club John went back to the secretary's office to report the intruders and for him to call the police. But when they entered the office they could hear the secretary groaning. Between them they carefully lifted him back into his chair and he was obviously very poorly and quite dazed. John used the office phone to call the police and report the savage attack. He advised that they get to the Club as quickly as possible and that the perpetrators were now locked in the men's shower-room. They made the secretary as comfortable as they could and poured him a glass of water, before they left the building and made their way to the Marina.

It did not take them long to find 'Sunrise' bobbing gentle at her mooring. They soon had their gear stowed away. John started the engine, eased the boat from the floating dock, and headed towards the sea. At the same time looking up at the mast to check that all was well with the rigging. He then turned on the VHF radio and tuned into channel 14. He picked up the mic and flicked the send switch 'Calling Lowestoft Harbour Master. Come in please' after a short pause the radio crackled into life

'This is the Lowestoft Harbour Control, please give the name of your boat and the passage you intend taking.'

'This is the 32ft sailing craft 'Sunrise' with two adults on board, sailing out of its home port of Lowestoft on a passage south along the east coast. We are expecting to make landfall at Ramsgate, Kent, sometime tomorrow afternoon. Before progressing to Cowes on the Isle of Wight the following day, Over'

'We confirm passage to Ramsgate, have a safe trip, over and out.'

With the nautical conventions sorted out John cast a last look back at the harbour and he was pleased to be able just pick out a police car parked outside the yacht club. They passed between the two piers at the entrance to the harbour and once clear John turned the boat south allowing plenty of distance between them and the stretch of shifting sandbank off the coast.

Janina had been sitting alongside him in the cockpit and had now taken off the large woollen hat they had been using as a part disguise – now her thick long blond hair flowed back over her shoulder. Quite a sight thought John.

'So, now we do have an engine John'

'Yes, engine, plastic boat, electric lights, fairly modern navigation equipment, but she is still a nice steady boat, not a racer but strong and easy to sail. The engine will not be running for much longer, I don't want to waste this lively sea breeze.

You take over the tiller, just keep it centred for the time being while I raise the sails. Then we can sit down, take stock of where we are, and think about the next stage of our journey.'

The word 'adventure' nearly slipped out instead of 'journey' showing his feelings about at last again facing 'bad guys', just as he had during his time in the army and then the police.

It did not take him long to raise the mainsail and hank on and raise the number 2 Genoa – bit too lively for the number 1 he judged. Back in the cockpit he set the sail with a decent wind coming over their stern port quarter. He let the main run out and gave the Genoa sufficient slack sheeting to fill. The boat responded immediately, surging forward as he bent down to the control panel and cut the engine.

Above them wide-winged gulls were taking advantage of the thermals to drift in lazy circles high in the sky while a line of Oystercatchers called their plaintive cry as they flew towards the land.

'My goodness I am hungry' said John 'Time for a late lunch.'

'OK, you stay here and I will see what I can come up with from the kitchen' – 'Galley!' John corrected her.

'The parts of boats often have very different names to similar parts of houses and other forms of transport. Oh, and the toilets are the heads – left is port and right is starboard......don't worry I am sure that you will pick up the patios pretty soon, afterall, look how good your English is.'

'Yes, but I learn one version of English now you are telling me I have to learn another.' But she was smiling as she made her way down into the main cabin.

It didn't take long and Janina was back with thick cheese and tomato sandwiches and two mugs of tea. '

There seems to be quite a bit of food in the cupboards' 'Yes, that is typical of Chris he likes to keep the boat prepared to go at short notice, to our benefit.'

'When we have finished lunch I am going below for about half-an-hour so that I can plot our course..... This is something you would normally do before you set off, but our hasty departure prevented us from doing this'

'But who will steer the boat?'

'Don't worry Janina. You take the tiller and if you look at that compass on the control panel over the cabin door you can see that the vertical line is on 40 degrees, all you need to do is to roughly keep it set like this, just adjust the tiller if the line strays more than about 5 degrees left or right.'

'Port or starboard' she corrected with a smile.

'OK' said John returning the smile, 'Once we get into the trip we can set the auto-pilot for the easier stretches.'

Seated at the cabin's navigation table he was concentrating closely as he bent over the admiralty charts covering the east coast, a set of tide tables to hand. With a practised ease he manipulated the Hurst Plotter and a set of dividers, noting his calculations on an A5 pad. Some sailors would today look somewhat askance at John's use of such old-fashioned plotting methods, most would simply use GPS to outline a course. John preferred the challenge of using the traditional navigation methods. Although he did use his laptop to track weather patterns between the daily 5 pm shipping forecast on Radio 4, and also to assess up-to-date transits into each port.

Back in the cockpit, having trimmed the sails and adjusted the course, John took control of the tiller and sat back to enjoy the life-enhancing sense gained from skimming over the low-waved surface of the sea as the boat was driven south by wind-filled sails.

Over a hundred miles away in Argyle Square, Rahman had gathered leading members of his organization in his office, one of which was Florin.

He turned to Goldie his number two 'So, we seem to have had one fuck-up after another and no sign that we are going to catch up with Janina. We have a successful business, substantial profits on all fronts, we have a network of staffing that extends across Britain......and you pricks can't even track down a 22 year old girl on the run. So up-date us Goldie'

Goldie picked up on the subtle change from 'we have' for the successful organization to 'you can't even' for poor performance in the hunt for the girl. He was physically big, 6.4, and 18 stone of ex-heavy weight boxer taken to enforcement, where the lack of gentlemanly rules for fighting suited his aggressive nature much more so than the updated Queensbury Rules of boxing.

'What seemed to be a straight-forward track down and catch has been complicated by the girl tying up with some prick who can't seem to mind his own business, but who does seem to be able to handle himself. Due to our contacts in the Met. we have been able use his van registration to identify this guy - John Hardy – He is ex-marine/special forces and police service in SCO19, so not surprising that he is quite good. But he should not have been good enough to make complete dicks out of an armed Florin and Mihai, supported by a local team.'

Florin had kept his head down during this assessment taking a great interest in the office carpet – he knew that it was unlikely that there would not be a consequence due to his failure.

'We have Mihai and a local staff member being charged with GBH with a possible murder charge if the guy they bashed does not pull through. It looks like a jail sentence for sure, with Mihai being deported at the end of his. Our tame Q.C. has already travelled up to Suffolk Police headquarters to see what he can do.'

Ashif raised his hand and Goldie paused.

'Wake up you lot – you need to be seriously alert from now as we plan our next move....I would say that we have had enough pissing around. I want the diamonds, the money, and the notebook here within a week, as to the girl, she can be dead.'

Goldie continued with his assessment. 'After screwing our guys in the town of Lowestoft it seems that they have stolen or borrowed a boat and have headed out of the harbour. They could have gone north, south, or even straight across the channel to France or Belgium. ......Basically, they could have gone any fucking where. One of our local staff, a Rees, who had been with Florin, seems to know a bit about this sailing lark and he reckons that the Harbour Office would have a record of the destinations of all boats leaving the harbour. This is information they would not provide on request so Rees says that him and his mate intend visiting the office late tonight when there is only one officer on duty and he reckons he could get the information we want. Mind you, this would assume that this John guy did not lie about their destination in case we found out.'

Goldie looked to his boss who had already unfolded a map of Britain and spread it out on his ornate desk.

'One way or another, we need to get these two.......for now alert your operatives in all the major cities and say that there will be a 20K bonus for whoever finds them. If we do hear back from Rees about their destination we can narrow the focus for the search.'

'Florin, you fuck off and maintain contact with this Rees and before you go hand over the Koch, it costs too much for you to hang on too. Oh and bear in mind that you have seriously stretched my patience so you have a lot of ground to make up......just now your credibility account as an operative in the organization is seriously in deficit.'

'Let's move on to the next business, Irvin you report first'

And so the mob's meeting continued with reports from each of the senior operatives: prostitution, clubs, the protection racket-stroke insurance business. Then they turned to the two casinos, profitable in themselves but also used to launder the dirty proceeds of crime into clean new money with its past washed away within these seemingly legitimate gambling enterprises.

'So all good with these...... What is this I have been hearing about an issue with drugs, your area Kurt, what's the problem?'

'No problem with supply' said Kurt, a particularly ugly specimen with blue, red, and black, Maori-style tattoos on his left cheek around his left eye and across the top of a shaven head.

'For weed we are continuing with our mutually satisfactory arrangement with the Philippino net-work in the UK that mostly uses illegal immigrants to grow the plants in rented houses. Then we buy off them, and process and distribute as required. A nicely smooth operation'

'For cocaine, the shipping route from Columbia to Lisbon or Bilbao and then by private jet to Biggin Hill airport continues unmolested. It was genius to use Biggin Hill boss. It is becoming an exclusive location for the very richest to come into London by hired or personally owned jet. Searches are almost always cursory and if they do on occasion use the drug dogs, then one of the airport staff who is on our payroll tips us off and the pilot parks some way from the terminal and we then do a rapid unload before customs can get to the plane.

We are currently importing 30 kilos a week on this route. As you know the goods are then moved from the airport to two nearby but separate industrial units where the parcelling out takes place and distribution made to our leading operatives in each of the regions that we control. With further processing and local distribution taking place at the regional units.

This is all good.

We still use the traditional route by mules from Jamaica through UK customs, with stomachs stuffed with the goods – but this does currently have a 20% detection rate. Not that much of a problem for us as the Columbian cartel accepts our estimates of losses and allows for this in the price. And of course, those caught are dispensable, so on their own.'

Ashif looked up 'If no problem with supply then its distribution presumably.'

'Not really' said Kurt becoming nervous about how he would explain the problem,

'We do have another organization, more just a bunch of juvenile gangsters, who are trying to muscle in on the trade in the southwest.'

'So nothing new' said Ashif. 'We just incorporate the brightest of any such gang into our organization and deter the rest, if necessary by violence.'

'Yes agreed, but these seem to be a particularly tough bunch, seemingly quite well organised and hard to identify, but don't worry it is in hand I just want permission to draw fire-power as this could get nasty before it gets sorted out.'

'What is the extent of the competition so far?'

'Well, it seems to be mainly centred on the cities of Plymouth and Exeter, and as you know, these are centres of control for the trade across Devon and Cornwall. The worst loss so far has been half a million lost during a raid on our monthly exchange at the Fleet Services, and last week a month's supply of drugs.....'

Rahman held up his hand. 'Are you fucking telling me that we have lost over a million pounds worth of money and goods and you just describe them as "Just a bunch of gangsters" Christ think of our reputation.'

A chastened Kurt replied. 'Sorry boss I was thinking in terms of how we deal with it'

'So I hope you are going to tell me that our own security are either all dead or are very badly injured in their attempt to prevent these two raids'

'So far the main confrontations have been at Fleet Services when one of our operatives suffered a bad head injury and a broken collar bone and the other a broken foot. Then at the unit in Exeter, one of our security guards collected a bellyful of shotgun pellets and another being barrel-whipped when the drugs were taken. So far I admit we are struggling to find out who the gang are. We have tried to collate information from our operatives at the Fleet and Exeter incidents and as far as we can determine there are four of them and they all seem to be late teens early twenties. So it looks like this bunch of arseholes have just gotten lucky and we should be able to track them down. They will have to be wasted otherwise our credibility could suffer. Our leading operative in the south-west, Carl Kimble, suggests that they could use a bit of help in this pest control.'

'I am seriously pissed off with our security Kurt – What with these raids and the fucking farce off the east coast, it looks like we are becoming soft – too complacent, and we need to crackdown very hard and very soon........There is never a shortage of tin-pot gangs who think they are ready to step up from pimping, burglary, and car crime, to the men's game of serious drug supply, so another bunch of wankers to stamp down hard on Kurt, an example to others in that area who might have similar ideas.....I will contact Benny at the Park Royal warehouse and tell him to book out whatever fire-power you think would be useful, oh and you can have this Koch pistol for a start, that should deter anyone who it is pointed at in anger.'

The sail down the east coast was going well for John and Janina. The wind had steadily shifted to the south-east and in response John exchanged the Genoa for a number 1 Jib and when back in the cockpit he hardened the sails, steering as close into the wind as the design of the boat would allow.

'This is just about the fastest point of sailing' said John. He moved the tiller as small adjustments became necessary and in doing could feel the exhilarating power of a sailing boat surging through the water.

By mid-afternoon they were passing across the wide Thames Estuary and Janina asked about the odd-looking large metal structures, seemingly abandoned in the sea.

'They are called Maunsell forts after Guy Maunsell the designer. Built during World War II to protect the entrance to the river.... I think there were originally about nine of them spread across the estuary but, due to neglect and, for some due to collisions with boats on foggy days, only a few have survived. Each one used to house up to about 250 men – Their job being to maintain and man anti-aircraft guns as well as some more substantial cannons.'

'They do look quite spooky with their rusty hulks atop of those animal-like legs rising from the sea.' Said Janina

'Yes, I think they have used them in sci-fi films in the past' said John as he continued with his history lesson.

'Oddly, a couple of them did have quite a colourful time in the 1960s after being decommissioned as military establishments. This was as bases for pirate, meaning unlicensed, radio stations, broadcasting pop music to mainland Britain. I do remember that one of the radio stations was run by a guy called David Sutch, who used the name 'Screaming Lord Sutch'. He stood out in the drab early 1960s as quite a character. A minor musician himself but a lively and well liked D.J. He also had another life as a politician of sorts. He led a subversive political party called 'The Monster Raving Loony Party'. It had a mixed membership composed of the quaint, the quirky, the perverse, and the downright deranged. Mind you, it was a party that, in effect, stuck two fingers up to the establishment. So in some ways it was a useful addition to the British political scene. They did have some unusual, indeed outrageous policies...... I seem to remember that they advocated the legalisation of drugs, and that the National Debt was to be cleared by putting it on a national credit card, another policy was that half of the grey squirrel population should be painted red to increase red squirrel numbers and Zebra crossings were to be used for any animal wishing to cross the roads. Mind you, they also advocated Britain leaving the European Common Market as it was then called pre–European Community days. And today, in 2010, there seems to be some gathering mainstream pressure to achieve this.'

'Wow' exclaimed Janina 'How do you know this type of stuff, you would not have been born in the 1960s?'

'Yes, but Lord Sutch was politically active throughout the 1980s when I was a teenager. And bear in mind Janina, I have always been a keen reader. An unfortunate side effect of this being that you pick up a mass of pretty useless information that trails through life with you. Give it about 20 years and you will probably be in a similar.... brain full of 'random stuff' condition. In the meantime let's have cup of coffee.'

They sailed on, crossing the estuary and then making good progress along the south east coast under a lowering sky, with the sea now a deep blue-gray after the dirty brown-gray water of the estuary.

John passed the tiller over to Janina and went below just to double-check his calculations on their passage. He knew they were approaching the notorious 'Goodwin Sands', a 10 mile long 3 mile wide stretch of sandbank off the coast of Kent. He was aware that about 2,000 boats had been noted as being sunk on the treacherous sands since records began in about 1300 C.E. During one infamous night in 1703, a fleet of 13 men-of-war, along with 40 merchant vessels, were sheltering in the narrow channel between the coast and the sandbank known as 'The Downs'. But the storm was so fierce that most of the ships were blown onto the shallow sands where they were exposed to the crashing waves and soon broke up, with 2,168 seamen losing their lives. Even though he knew that there had not been a fatal incident on the Sands for the past fifty years John still felt that it was best to double-check his navigation.

Having satisfied himself that they were sailing safely wide of the Sands he turned to focusing on coming into Ramsgate Harbour just 6 miles further on. About half a mile out he started the engine, lowered the main mainsail, and removed and stowed the jib. He then used channel 14 on the VHF radio to call up the Ramsgate Port Control, provide details of his boat and to ask permission to enter the port. This being granted, he motored into the outer harbour and then passed the modest lighthouse on the port-side sea wall of the inner harbour. Tuning the radio to channel 80 he called up the Marina Office to be directed to an overnight visitor's berth. Once securely moored for the night he took a mop to the decks and more generally gave the boat a clean-up whilst Janina made a start on cooking their dinner.

Within half-an-hour they were sitting at the galley table enjoying spaghetti and meat balls and sharing a bottle of Chianti that John felt sure his friend Chris would not mind him taking from the boat's modest store of wine.

It was bit later over coffee, when seated on the comfortable settee in the main cabin, that John asked Janina to continue with her story, one that was becoming a story of escape rather than of imprisonment.

Janina – breathed deeply then picked up her tale. 'Well, there I was determined to escape, and thanks to Kay, I could now leave the room. The next barrier would be the two guards downstairs in the reception area who I knew from experience, would be either watching the constantly on T.V. or fiddling with their mobile phones.

I thought that I would need some money, and being aware that it was too early in the day for Rahman to be there, I went down to his first floor office where I had seen the thick wad of money in the desk draw. When I slid the draw open I could see the money along with the bag containing the diamonds, and as a last thought I also took the notebook, assuming that it could be valuable as it had been kept with the money and diamonds. It just shows the arrogance of Rahman to have such weak security in his headquarters.

But then I still had to get past the security in reception. As I walked gingerly along the first floor corridor a door opened and a heavily made up and scantily dressed women emerged just in front of me. She went down the stairs with quite a swagger and I assumed that she then left the hotel.

Creeping careful down the stairs, I was able to see through the fan-light at the top of the door into the reception area. One of the guards was standing by the door idly looking over the Square whilst the other one was fiddling with his phone. I did not recognise either of these so thought that they would not know what I looked like. This, and seeing the women just before in the corridor gave me an idea.

I went back to my bedroom – pretty much smothered my face with garish makeup, hiked my skirt up as far as I could to expose my legs and opened the top buttons of my blouse to show plenty of cleavage. During my time as a prisoner I had been able to hear women that Kay had explained were prostitutes discussing their business so I was confident I could assume their style of talking. I looked into the mirror and practised the phases

'You looking for some company love?' and 'That punter was a fucking good trick' a few times.

Thinking that, although the phrases themselves would not help me get past the guards the same casual off-hand style of talking just might. I stuffed a bag with the bits taken from Rahman's office, and some underwear, before lifting this onto my shoulder. I pulled on a baseball cap, tilted it over one side of my face and managed an half-hearted grin at my reflection as I embarked on what I hoped would my escape.

Sorry about the detail John but describing this to you feels like a sort of counselling session, allowing me to absorb and make sense of the crazy experience of my last few weeks.

My heart was pounding as I made my way back down to the reception. I slowly counted to five and pushed open the door. The two bored looking guards looked up as I endeavoured to swagger past. The one leaning against the door-frame remarked that he hadn't seen me before and asked if I was new. 'New to the Square but not new to the fucking game love' I said in a feisty style that I hoped suited my role.

I could feel his eyes on me as I tripped my way down the outside steps and along the Square towards the main road. When I reached the main road I managed to catch a black cab and asked the driver to take me to Liverpool Street Station.'

'Why Liverpool Street?' John interrupted. 'You would have had St Pancras and King Cross just a few hundred yards away.'

'Yes, but I thought that Rahman would assume that I would take the Euro train from St Pancras or even a train out of London from the nearby Kings Cross. And I was thinking that the trains from Liverpool Street would go to the city of Liverpool. A city I had read about as the birthplace of the Beatles and the home of the famous Liverpool Football Club – The impression gained from Lithuanian TV was of Liverpool being a substantial port with lots of friendly people. But of course, when I tried to buy a ticket to Liverpool I was told I would need to go by underground to King Cross. I was certain that my absence would soon be noticed, and Kings Cross would probably be one of the first places where they would be looking for me. Unsure what to do I glanced up at the train departure times and saw that a train was leaving for Norwich in just five minutes.

So, I bought a First-Class ticket courtesy of Rahman. And, although I received some strange looks from other passengers and a query from a train guard about my being in First Class, my swagger returned, and I soon found a comfortable window seat in a compartment and then set to work to remove some of the makeup and adjust my clothes to a more modest level of exposed flesh.

I was quite excited by my successful escape and thought that the money and diamonds would offer some compensation for what I had endured. But I also realized that I would soon be pursued by some very bad men. I considered my options. The police seemed to be obvious but after what Kay had said about Rahman's cosy relationship with some officers in the London police, I was afraid of this. I thought that I should be able to find a route back to Lithuania.

When we arrived at Norwich I seemed to have arrived at a terminal with only limited options for onward travel. One of these was the line out of the city to Great Yarmouth. When I asked her what Great Yarmouth was like, a friendly lady processing tickets told me that it was quite a nice seaside town, if it did also have a rather rundown port area. The idea of its being a port was a positive for me. I thought that surely I would be able to obtain a passage across the channel to Belgium or France. So I bought a ticket and was soon travelling east out of the city.

During this journey I started to feel very sweaty and was shaking uncontrollably. I now think I had a form of shock caused by the stress of planning and making my escape following four weeks of imprisonment. When the train stopped at the village of Acle I was panicking and felt that I just had to have a walk in the open air. I thought that I could just continue my journey on a later train.

Walking though the village I began to feel even worse and also quite tired. That's when I saw the hotel and I thought that I could spend the night, shower, and get back on a train the next day. Within an hour I was showered and settled down in my room when I was startled by the ringing of the mobile phone that had been given to me. A phone that I had forgotten about, it being one was I could not call out on, one that was only used to receive daily calls from Rahman. This was him and he was shouting all sorts on vile stuff down the phone. He said that he would have me tracked down and would personally strangle me. I cut the call and threw the phone into the bed. I was by then feeling pretty ragged. I just sat on the edge of the bed nervously contemplating the poor prospects for my immediate future.

That's when I saw your van drive into the car-park John. If you remember after parking you got out of the van and walked around in the car park as if stretching your legs. There was something about you that drew me – you reminded me of a cousin I spent a lot of time with as a child. A cousin now working in Canada as an agronomist. It was raining and I saw you put your smiling face up to the rain rather than rush to get back into the van and this tiny action gave me a sense of an unusual person.

During the next few hours I was now becoming progressively more desperate, all sorts of horrible thoughts were passing through my mind. I was in such a panic......and that is when I rushed out of the hotel, without even putting on my shoes, and approached your van that night John. And we do know that two of Rahman's men arrived at the hotel soon after – presumably they had been able to locate my phone......So that's it John, my journey from my quiet life in Lithuania to a small village in Norfolk, and I really do feel so much better for having been able to tell you all about it......And I should thank you for saving my life!'

'Well, thanks for sharing your story with me Janina, I think we have a way to go yet before we can feel safe but it's midnight now and it has been quite a long day's sailing today, so let's get a good night's sleep and get ready to go again tomorrow.'

As they settled down to sleep 120 miles to the north Rees and Jimmy were knocking on the door of Lowestoft Harbour Control Office. On entering they found a formidable looking women in a dark blue harbour master's uniform sitting at a radio control panel on a desk set in front of a wide bay window overlooking the harbour.

'Just proceed forward into the inner harbour please Kestrel, over and out.'

Hanging up her microphone the woman turned to these two. 'Yes' What can I do for you?'

'We want to know the destination of a boat that left Lowestoft about 10 am this morning.'

The Harbour Master shook her head dismissively, 'Our records of boat movements are confidential, so sorry but I can't disclose this information.'

Hearing this, Jimmy pulled out a nasty looking knife and held it to the woman's throat.

'Look lady we are not pissing about, either you give us the information or I will slit your fucking throat'

The Harbour Master held up her left hand and with the right picked up and made as if to pass a large folder that had been on the desk to Jimmy but instead used it to try to knock the knife from his hand. Rees stepped forward and hit the woman hard on her shoulder with a baseball bat that he had been holding down by his side. The woman collapsed onto the floor crying in pain. 'Stupid bitch,' said Rees 'Let's get that folder and get out of here.'

They ran to a waiting car.... getting in Jimmy ordered their driver to get moving. Once on the road back to Great Yarmouth Rees flicked quickly through the folder to today's date. He ran his finger down the list of boats leaving that morning. 'Look there were only two boats leaving the harbour between 9.30 and 10.30 this morning, one was named 'Snow Goose' and the other was 'Sunrise'. It says here that 'Snow Goose' had a crew of six whereas 'Sunrise' only had two people on board...so that's our target.' He quickly made a call to the Argyle Square office and informed them that the couple they were chasing had given their destination as Cowes on the Isle of Weight, but that they intended stopping over-night in Ramsgate, a port on the south coast of England.

Goldie took the call from Rees and he immediately called Ashif to pass on the news and to clarify the next step. Ashif said he would be at the office within the next hour and that Goldie was to call in three of their best operatives for a meeting.

'Tell them to pack for spending three/four nights away.'

He also gave a list of weaponry tthat he would arrange to be delivered to the hotel from the Park Royal store. And in the meantime, he told Goldie to work on a plan of intervention.

By 2am the air in the office was steadily filling with pungent cigarette smoke. Goldie was standing by the window, two very hard looking men in their mid 40s were on the settee and on a stool by the desk was seated a women whose glance most people would not want to hold to in a pub. The two men were fairly standard operatives in the higher echelons of the organization. One, Joe, was ex-British army, dismissed at the age of nineteen after only one year of service due to a psychological assessment made following in incident where an innocent civilian was killed in Northern Ireland. He then saw service as a mercenary in Rhodesia where he met his colleague Irvin, who was then serving in the notorious Selous Scouts. Both, when in their early 20s, had been engaged in the often gruesome activity of hunting down soldiers of the two rebel forces fighting for independence from white minority rule. The NLA led by Robert Mugabe and the PRA led by Joshua Nkomo.

Joe and Irvin had fought against fighters for freedom, or rather had fought simply for the pay and perversely for the enjoyment of conflict. But the women, Zerya, had from her early teenage years been fighting for the Kurdish Workers Party (PPK) against the Turkish and Iraqi regimes as her people, the Kurds, sought an independent state of their own. Nearly two decades of living a hard, lonely, life in mainly dessert conditions, peppered by occasional bloody clashes with troops from Turkey or Iraq, had turned a young idealistic girl into a cold-hearted Amazonian warrior. One now able to maim or kill without a second thought, other than of the going rate of pay ....and for her the steady and generous pay received from Ashif was sufficient to buy her loyalty and her intimidating physical skills.

Ashif came into the room and his presence immediately raised the alertness of the others as he told Goldie to unfold the map of Britain and spread it on the desk. 'Right' Ashif said 'We now have a serious issue. I had assumed that Florin and Mihai, aided by our operatives in the east of the country would quite easily catch and return Janina along with the goods she has stolen from me.

Now my first thought was that they were over-rated pricks that were not up to the job. But, as I mentioned at an earlier meeting when three of you were not present, we have now gained information about the guy that Janina as hooked up with - his name is John Hardy - and it does seem that she has by some unfortunate coincidence found a fucking white knight. A man with some quite formidable physical skills who we now have to assume is carrying a Koch pistol lost by Mihai – from now we will be treating him as serious opposition.'

Joe looked a bit confused. 'So Joe, do you have something to say?'

'No boss, it was just a surprise to think of one man could be a serious opposition for us.'

'That attitude, of underrating him, was exactly the mistake Florin and Mihai made......You four need to learn from their error'.

'Our informant in the Met. police traced the van the couple were using to this Hardy and once he had the guy's name and address he was able to gain information that he recently retired from the police SCO19, so an experienced firearms officer, and that before joining the police he had served ten years in the Marines serving, apparently with distinction, in various Middle Eastern locations. Hopefully hearing this will show the need to treat him as serious opposition.'

The group gathered round the desk as Goldie briefed them on the currently assessed whereabouts of John and Janina, and outlined an action plan.

'Our information is that they should be spending tonight in the south coast town of Ramsgate and tomorrow sailing on to Cowes, a port on the Isle of Wight.'

'Right, let's get going' said Irvin, his preferring action to much planning detail.

'No, we will not be taking them in Ramsgate. They would be in a very public place, and we don't have any local operatives who are familiar with the port area. We do trade there of course, but this is outreach from Dover. Instead we will be taking them in Cowes. I have already alerted our operatives in Southampton and two of them will be crossing on the ferry to the Island early tomorrow morning to make sure that the number of marinas that they could be stopping in can be covered.' Any questions so far? Yes Zerya?'

'What is the preferred outcome of this operation?'

'Just like you Zarya to get straight to the nub of what is expected....' Said Ashif.

'Ideally, it would be return of the money, diamonds, and notebook, with two badly mutilated bodies either dumped on the Island or disposed of in the sea. A minimum would be the return of the notebook and two bodies.... If I was being really fussy, I would like the ideal option just noted but with Janina being brought to me so that I can personally bring her life to a very painful end'

Following this blunt clarification, they turned back to consider the map.

Goldie continued.....'Once the four of us are on the Island we will be a force of six, and the boss has arranged for sufficient firepower for us invade the bloody Island, let alone deal with just two people. This gear should be here within an hour – so get some sleep now and we will liaise here at ten o'clock tomorrow, check out the weapons and be on the road by eleven. Two places have been booked on the car ferry from Southampton to Cowes for 2pm. We will take two Range Rovers, Jo and Irvin in one, and Zerya and me in the other.'

Zerya, Jo, and Irvin went to get their heads down for a few hours leaving Goldie and Ashif in the office.

'I think I have a lesson to learn here Goldie....We have a really profitable business model with the occasional opposition being easily neutralised. We also have some useful contacts with senior officers of the both the Met. and some local forces. But now, due to my wish to procreate in a particular way we now have this potentially awkward distraction........I do wish to be able to pass on the business but perhaps I should just seek to keep growing richer and then retire gracefully, leaving the running and eventually even the ownership of the business to a trusted individual, such as yourself.'

'I am not going to argue with that option boss but let's plan on any retirement being well into the future.'

Chapter Three

In Ramsgate the early morning sun was casting long shadows as well as its warmth over the Marina. The plaintive calling of numerous sea-gulls was the most obvious sound, if in the back-ground was the increasing noise of traffic signally an, if modest, rush hour. One more obvious further into the slowly waking town. Even at this early hour a few sailing and motor boats were nudging their way out of the harbour, most no doubt looking forward to a day ahead being spent on the water.

John and Janina were sitting in the cockpit of Sunrise enjoying coffee with the money, diamonds, and the notebook that she had taken from Rahman's office set out on a small table.

'I have been taking a closer look through the notebook Janina, and its content looks like dynamite. There is sufficient information here involving police and political corruption to cause considerable damage. But it also shows the power that Rahman's organization must have. There are named officers, not just in the Met but also in county forces.'

This did not mean much to Janina but she posed the question

'What I can't understand when I overheard Rahman and his number two, Goldie, laughingly taking about these as being 'blood diamonds', is that some term for noting the quality of diamonds?'

'I think I can answer that, an answer that would have nothing to do with assessing diamonds for their quality. Quality is more about the 4c's colour, cut, clarity, carat. I think that the 'blood' refers to the human cost of trading these stones. A number of African countries have highly productive diamond mining areas. Indeed diamonds, along with gold and slaves, were at least part of the 19th century drive to colonize Africa. A resource rich continent that has been reduced to poverty by two centuries of relentless forms of economic colonisation and too often the collusion of greedy African leaders.

The extensive diamond mining that is carried out in conflict zones in countries such as Angola, Liberia, and Sierra Leone, often provide a means to fund civil conflict, and indeed to line the pockets of leading local politicians. I served alongside a young guy whose family had fled Sierra Leone, and even back then in the early 1990s he said that the weapons used by each side in the civil war were often paid for by illegally sold diamonds. These are sold with the collusion of some western governments prepared to take a pretty loose approach to monitoring the end-use of arms manufactured and sold by companies in their jurisdiction.

A sales process that often involves serial ownership passing through layers of paper companies and a number of shady agents, before they arrived in a war zone. Even the very process of diamond mining causes damage to the local population, turning fertile farmland into desolate wasteland, and poisoning ground water. The craters left as mines move on become ponds of stagnant water providing breeding conditions suitable for malaria carrying mosquitoes. So you can see that 'blood diamonds' is an appropriate name for these.'

Janina scooped up the small bag of diamonds and made to throw them into the water. 'No' said John grabbing her wrist.

'I can understand how you feel towards these their being tainted with the blood of Africans but we can hopefully find a legitimate buyer and can use the money gained for good, perhaps send to an African orphanage......it would be a positive that can perhaps come from evil.

We have become entangled with an extensive organization – I had thought that they were just a bunch of thugs but from what Kay told you, your own experience, and what this notebook shows, this must just about be the most extensive criminal gang operating in the UK today.

We will need to bring in the authorities at some point, and I do have a contact that I am sure I can trust, but I want to think about possible ways forward before making contact. I think we have lost the bad guys for the time being.

For now, I need to call into the Marina Office to pay for last night's stay. It will be another four hours until the tide turns, and so for us to be able to make an easier start to a passage west along the south coast. So let's have a look around the town, grab some lunch, and aim to set off about oneish.'

It did not take them long to clear the breakfast things away and make their way to the town quay and up the steps to the Marina Office. While paying the mooring fee, John overheard an obviously sailing type, fashionably dressed, in 'Henri-Lloyd' sailing shorts and light zipper jacket, talking into a mobile phone 'Yes Martin, I should be in Hamble Marina by about eight this evening, the heavy weather noted in last night's shipping forecast is not due to come in from the west until late Monday.' 'Shit', thought John 'How rusty am I'

When cruising at sea tuning into the 5 pm shipping forecast was pretty much a must do, and it had slipped his mind. But then he reasoned that they should be comfortably tied up in the shelter of Cowes later today and, it being Saturday, they still had another day or so to sail further before the need to find shelter from the predicted storm.

Walking around in the town Janina was wide-eyed at the variety of goods available in the large number of small shops lining the High Street and the smaller streets leading from this. Yes, since the break-up of the Soviet Union and the opening up of the economies of the Baltic States, there was much more to buy in Lithuania's shops and markets, but nothing like even here in a small English town.

John led her into a chandlery store with its rows of shelves tightly packed with all sorts of marine equipment and boat maintenance products. There were racks of drums wound with multi-coloured cords and ropes of varying thickness. And a range of white or blue plastic fenders were hanging from the ceiling. He guided Janina towards the back of the shop where he saw that the sailing clothes were on show. 'Here, try this on' he said, taking down a bright yellow suit. 'You might need this if we do encounter heavy weather. I can use the one Chris keeps on board.'

'It's a bit bright, isn't it?'

'All the better to see you my girl if you do get tipped into a heavy sea...... That's the point of the colour.'

Janina was working herself into the fairly heavy one-piece suit with attached boots when she saw the cost. '£600!! how can that be, this is a more than a month's pay in Lithuania.'

'Yes, but the cost reflects the work that goes into these. We know them as dry-suits, if traditional sailors still call them 'oilies' short for oil-skins, but they could easily be named survival-suits, as they could be the difference between life and death if you find yourself in cold water for more than 30 or so minutes, when hypothermia could take hold.'

In addition to the dry-suit he also included two sets of polypropylene thermal underwear, two pairs of thermal socks, and a sailing balaclava each with the final load they carted to the pay desk. John drew out his co-op credit card but Janina slapped twenty £50 notes onto the counter –

'If necessary we will survive the seas thanks to Rahman's generosity!'

This made sense to John and with his credit still healthy they left the shop and were soon sitting at a table on the terrace of a boutique style restaurant situated within a picturesque row of affluent-looking regency houses overlooking the harbour.

Having eaten quite a light salad lunch John put in a call to his ex-colleague Bill 'Nobby' Graveny, who was a Detective Chief Superintendent in the Met's serious crime squad. A gruff voice came on the line 'Graveny here...' 'Hi Nobby, its John Hardy here, can you talk?'

'Sure just working through some witness statements on a local drive-by shooting, it's always disappointing how little witnesses see when drugs wars are involved and fear of retribution freezes memories. Anyway, how's things John, I guess it's all cardigans, carpet slippers, and log fires for you now.'

'Yea stuff you too...I seem to have gotten myself involved with a bit of a problem and need to at least have your view. You work in serious crime in London and I know you are a straight copper.'

'Why do you say that' interrupted Bill

'I can't go into all the details now Nobby but suffice to say that I have got myself into quite a challenging situation involving a London-based criminal organization and I have evidence that they have extensively infiltrated the Met.'

'Unfortunately John, corruption in the Met. is nothing new..... but to be fair, the new commissioner is attempting a piecemeal approach to clear the shit from the Augean stable. The main problem being the unofficial pact of silence...... and even if an officer is not themselves involved in corruption they are wary of raising suspicions about senior officers that might resent even just being investigated. More recently, any formal investigations that have taken place have only positively identified low grade officers. Those paid just to look the other way when passing brothels and cannabis houses. The few investigations that have been attempted involving more senior officers have invariably failed due to the lack of hard evidence. You can't sack a senior police officer on suspicion alone, and an officer that has been unsuccessfully investigated can bear a serious grudge against those he or she judged to have reported them...... Anyway, you did not phone to hear what you pretty much already knew, how can I help?'

'If we can pull off a plan I am working on then I think I can provide solid evidence that could make the Met. stable shine brightly and even smell nice!.....in the meantime I am seeking all the information I can find of a criminal named Ashif Rahman, sometimes known as B..... 'Big Man' interrupted Bill, he blew out his cheek...'Christ John, if you are at the wrong end of dealing with this guy then your phrase of it being a 'challenge' is somewhat of an understatement'...... there was a pause on the line… 'Are you still there Nobby?' asked John. 'Yes, sorry John, I was just thinking about the implications of your situation. Rahman is the head of what is undoubtedly the biggest criminal organization in Britain. His organization is a type of British Mafia – protection racket, prostitution and the related women trafficking, drug smuggling and distribution, dodgy casinos, and more recently we suspect involvement in illegal blood diamond trading. And, in progressing these activities, we know of serial witness intimidation and the use of severe violence to the point of murder. A thoroughly nasty piece of work, with access to the best accountants and lawyers.....phew John, if you have crossed this guy then you do have what you modestly described as a challenge on your hands.

The serious crime squad has tried time and again to pin a serious crime that we know Rahman, or one of his lieutenants, was personally involved in, but he always seem to be one step ahead of us......which bring us back to the corrupt senior officers John – the bastard has access to inside information........Leave it with me John, I will see what I can dig up – If you think you have information that can expose corrupt serving Met. officers and can provide evidence to lock Rahman and his henchmen up for a long time, then I am sure that the commissioner will want to take a close personal interest. I will ask for a one-to-one meeting with her..... I will call you as soon as arrangements have been made in relation to how best we can progress this matter John'

'Thanks Nobby, take care'…

'It more important that you take care John – and do call me if an emergency, I would like to think that I could gather at least three or four SCS officers at short notice if required.'

While John had been making the call, Janina was using the time to feed a couple of sparrows with crumbs from left-over bread rolls. 'They look to be pretty plump little sparrows' he observed 'they must be regulars here.'

'Zvirbulis' exclaimed Janina 'Don't tell me... that is Lithuanian for sparrow' he said, remembering the recent experience with the octopus in the aquarium.

'I am becoming fluent in Lithuanian. That will be useful if one day I visit the country.' 'I really hope that one day you will John' said a serious looking Janina.

The pair returned to Sunrise and within half an hour they had stowed the new sailing gear and were motoring slowly out to the harbour mouth. John switched on the VHF radio selecting Channel 14 in order to check with Ramsgate Port Control that he was clear to leave the harbour and to give their destination as Cowes.

As the boat ventured from the shelter of the harbour into the Channel the more exposed conditions soon became apparent as the swell of the waves set the boat into a pattern of rising and falling as they made their way.

The wind was strongish (six on the Beaufort scale) and from the south so ideal for a fast broad-reaching passage along the south coast of Kent and on to Sussex and Hampshire. It did not take John long to raise the main-sail and go forward to hank on the nos.1 jib sail, while a now more confident Janina held the tiller on a steady course.

Meanwhile back in Argyle Square, the powerful V8 engines of two black Range Rovers were idling quietly as Joe, Irvin, and Zerya loaded the vehicles with their personal gear and the weaponry that has been issued to them. Goldie skipped lightly down the hotel steps to join them whilst Ashif stood at a first floor window looking on.

He felt a keen, more profession, interest in getting the notebook back, in the wrong hands this threatened his organization. The notebook was initially begun by Ashif's father and it was partly for sentimental reasons that he continued with this old fashioned method of record-keeping – the notebook contained details of payments made to corrupt politicians as well as senior Met officers and details of the leading operatives in each region of Britain,

But he was brimming with real anger, touching on madness, at the loss of Janina. As far as he was concerned, she had in effect signed her own death warrant when she had walked down the same steps taken just now by Goldie. He squeezed his sweaty hands tightly together as he imagined the feel of her neck between them.

The Range Rovers left the square, turned left into Grays Inn Road and then right into Pentonville Road, then it was on to City Road and a right turn onto the A10 Bishopsgate, before crossing the River Thames at London Bridge and continuing south to the set of roundabouts at the Elephant and Castle. Leaving these by the A3 Kennington Park Road, then following the A3 as it wound through south-west London and out to the suburbs. Within an hour they had crossed the busy M25, continuing on the A3 and by-passing Guildford – the prominent modern cathedral passing by unnoticed - before leaving the A3 and joining first the A31 then, just outside the city of Winchester joining the M3. Arriving at Southampton Dockside and the Red Funnel Ferry Terminal by one o'clock. During this two hour drive the two vehicles had maintained a 5 mile separation as a standard precaution. Two large black Range Rovers travelling in close convoy might just raise suspicions of police patrols or motorway cameras. And they had carefully observed all the traffic rules, even if holding the powerful Range Rovers down to 70 mph on the main roads was a challenge – the cruise control on each vehicle made this easier. This patience reflected their criminal professionalism. Only idiot criminals made themselves liable to get stopped by the police for something minor such as speeding, using mobile phones, or having an APR ping for their being uninsured. And then have a nosey traffic officer wanting to search the car, perhaps suspecting drugs or stolen goods. Having the guns found would not only be embarrassing it would also mean that they would have to shoot the officer. Un-necessary hassle and an interference with the main task they were supposed to be addressing. Ashif would be pissed if they made such an unprofessional error. And these four took a certain pride in their professional approach, whether this was in the killing itself or when making their way towards undertaking one.

The boat trip across the Solent only took about 40 minutes and the two cars were rolling down the lowered ramp of the ferry by 3 pm but to their surprise they had been offloaded onto the eastern side of the harbour when the main town was on the west side. 'Fuck it' said Goldie, who had spread the map out over the bonnet of his car 'It looks like we will have to drive all the way to the head of this fucking river to a town called Newport and then run up the other side to the town over there.'

'Still, observed Joe. 'If the targets left Ramsgate this morning, I doubt that they will be here until this evening at the earliest.'

They made their way along the two-lane road running beside the River Medina down to Newport and then taking another 30 minutes to run up to the main town of Cowes. Passing the extensive set of buildings of Albany and Parkhurst prisons.

'I think the Kray Twins served sentences in Parkhurst' said Jo, 'Couple of fucking amateurs leading a bunch of thick-headed east-end villains' suggested Goldie

Once they had driven down the hill into the affluent town it did not take long for them to find parking places on the quayside overlooking the wide entrance to Cowes harbour. With the prestigious 'Royal Yacht Sailing' and the 'Royal Yacht Squadron' clubs directly behind them. Irvin walked into the high street and returned with a selection of sandwiches and hot drinks and they sat on or stood by the low sea wall eating a late lunch. The four were surprised about the amount of boating activity on the water seen when crossing on the ferry and now being seen from the quayside. And on land, the harbour area itself was bustling with what were obviously sailing types with their wind-browned faces and colourful clothing.

They had arranged to meet up with a couple of the local contacts who had earlier in the day travelled over to the Island from Southampton to make a start on the search for Sunrise.

'Where are these dicks' asked Zerya.

Joe replied that he had 'Just had a text to say they would be here in five'

'The two men they had been expecting arrived and were quite red-faced, obviously having hurried to get there. One of them, Mick, said that he and his mate Craig had already made a start on looking through the Marina areas just to get some idea of their layouts but had found that these were considerably more extensive than they had thought.

'Listen up, this is the plan' said Goldie.

'Joe and Irvin will cross the harbour on the foot ferry, yes I know we only just left there but as we are not expecting them for a couple of hours you will in any case have some time to wait before you can begin a search. You Mick and Craig walk down this side of the harbour until you get to the marina furthest up the river. Zerya and I will buy a pair of binoculars from that shop over there and will hang around here and see if we can spot the boat as it comes in.'

'What about weapons?' asked Irvin. 'You and Joe take one Koch and a sawn-off shotgun. Craig and Mick take the same and that leaves us two with hand-guns. Make sure that you keep the shotguns in your coats. The barrels are short enough to allow this, and remember that if you do use them they will seriously harm anyone within a 3 foot arch when fired from 10 feet away. Collateral damage beyond our targets is OK if necessary, but best to avoid if possible.

Do not take them on unless success looks certain.....the Hardy guy can be killed however you want, he is totally disposable. Take the girl alive if possible but not a big deal if you kill her – the mark of success is our having the valuables and the notebook. Keep in touch every 15 minutes minimum. All clear?'

He noted a brief nod from each of the huddled group and he raised his hand in a signal to get them moving.

It was 7 pm before Sunrise was making its approach into the eastern channel at the entrance to Cowes Harbour. John and Janina had spent the day enjoying a lively sail in a south moving to south-easterly wind and also enjoying each other's company. They were coming together as a sailing team now and each moved easily around the boat. The journey had taken them round the coast of Kent and then Sussex where John had pointed out a bleak looking low spit of land jutting out into the sea.

'That spit of land has the unattractive name of Dungeness' said John, pointing to the land.

'It is a broad terrain of mostly pebbles that have over centuries been washed down the English Channel to form this expansive curl of land. It is much loved by birdwatchers due to the variety of birds species that are resident here, but even more so due to the rare birds that might stop off for a rest during their winter migration down the Channel. Using areas on the beaches and on the marshes behind them, to rest and feed before setting off again on their extended annual journey.'

'I suspect that your interest in birdlife, John, suggests you are perhaps a modest birdwatcher yourself'

'OK, I admit I do have an interest in all of the wildlife that surrounds us, on land, under the sea, and in the air – I think that years of sailing have brought me close to nature, and drawn me to it, and it into me. How can you not be amazed when you see a grey seal bob its head up from the sea or an otter do the same in a river, or the cerulean blue dragonfly when one settles on the rigging, and do you remember the majestic pair of Marsh Harriers we watched circling over us back on Breydon. I would admit to drawing an inner sense of calm from being able to enjoy such experiences.' He was by now gazing at the distant horizon, and continued

'I was once deployed to a Middle Eastern conflict zone – bombing had destroyed most local buildings and the roads were more a continuous series of craters than tarmac. People who had not fled were endeavouring to survive when food was scarce, water tainted, and the danger from the air was a constant concern.

We were engaged in clearing a village where we understood the enemy had dug in and were firing rockets at our base. During the sweep I dived behind a low wall in the face of heavy incoming fire and there crouched on the dusty ground was a young boy holding a small bird in his cupped hands. He held it up to me and smiled 'freedom' he said. Apart from my thinking that this was perhaps the only English word the boy knew, I immediately understood the boy was holding 'freedom' in his hands.....that he had seen the potential for freedom in the everyday. He raised his hands and released the bird. Here was a boy imprisoned in warfare, but he still knew what freedom meant. Every time I see a small bird or a butterfly in flight I think freedom is being expressed and what could be better....... Blimey Janina, look what you are doing.....bringing out the soppy in me. When my image is meant to be of a tough guy.... ex marine ex cop.'

She reached out and gently touched his hand. '

'No, that's nice, most women like to see a softer side in the men they are close too. And I am feeling evermore closer to you.'

Just then the loud blast of a boat-horn made them look up to see that they were on a course that would lead to a collision with a fishing boat with two deckhands engaged in hauling in its heavy net.

Following a short detour when avoiding the fishing boat they were soon back on course and within two hours they were just off the port city of Portsmouth with its obvious marker of the Spinnaker Tower high above the main city skyline. A giant architectural Jib-sail seeming to draw the city towards the sea.

Janina pointed to a number of low-lying solid brick structures in the water.

'Are they also forts like the ones we saw earlier, they don't have the long legs keeping the main building clear of the sea.'

'Yes and no' replied John. 'Yes, they are forts built to protect a part of England from sea-borne attack, but no they are not quite the same. These were built during the Napoleonic period when invasion from France was expected, whereas the Mausell forts protecting the Thames Estuary were built to defend against an expected invasion from Adolf Hitler's German army. The Mausell forts are constructed out of steel and iron, whereas these forts, known as the Solent Sea Forts, are built of stone. They each have a name – the one over by the entrance to Portsmouth Harbour is called The Spithead Fort, the one nearer to the Isle of Wight is called 'No Man's Land Fort' and the one in the middle is called 'Horse Sands Fort'. I think that one of these was sold recently and is being used as a private residence. And the 'Spithead Fort', the one with the red and white light-house has a luxury hotel on it. I think that you can even get married there.'

'You Brits seem to have ringed your little island with many military defences, your country is the animal equivalent of a prickly hedgehog as you face Europe. I am amazed that you know such detail as their names John.'

'Well, I would admit that these are marked on the sea-charts used to navigate through the Solent, so naming them was quite easy......And yes, this area of the south coast has seen significant military resources invested in defences over the centuries. It has become quite a tourist destination with various naval museums, and historic locations, including the dry dock containing HMS Victory, which was Nelson's flagship at the Battle of Trafalgar. It is interesting that Trafalgar, like the Battle of Waterloo ten years later, has made a significant contribution to British national mythology. The imaginative narrative that most nations construct or rather invent. Trafalgar is claimed to show the sailing skills, and the bravery and fighting ability of British sailors. But about half of the sailors in the British fleet were in fact foreigners. And, as for Waterloo, if the Prussian army had not turned up on that bleak day in 1815 then the British would probably have lost.'

'You seem to be quite cynical John, and yet you told me earlier that you served in the British Army'.

'Yes, I started out as a 19 year old Marine fired up with the idea of Queen and Country......keen to get out into the world to sort out the bad guys that threaten Britain. But I gradually came to realise that almost all activities involving the military of all sides threaten peace. In my time we went into the Middle East and mostly only managed to make bad situations even worse. I saw towns and cities left as rubble strewn bomb sites, what had been fertile farmland laid waste, and people's living conditions degraded or their lives prematurely ended – the sight of dead and wounded children was the hardest to take. The victory parades and medal award ceremonies seemed quite hollow affairs when I held the image of children's bodies in my mind.......that's why I left, I thought that I could do more good as a police officer than as a Marine.......

Anyway, changing the subject, over to starboard we have a city in Portsmouth that continues as an important base for the Royal Navy, but we won't be mooring in its Haslar Marina tonight. Instead we will now turn more to port and look for the marker for the eastern channel, taking us into Cowes'.

As they entered the channel John had lowered the main sail and stowed the Jib. He called up the Cowes Harbour Masters office on VHF channel 69, its local radio bandwidth, just to confirm arrival and to ask permission to enter the harbour. This given, he then called up the East Cowes Marina to book an overnight mooring. On their port side they were passing the car ferry landing stage just as a bright Red Funnel line boat was heading back across the Solent.

John had decided to forgo mooring at the more obvious marinas closest to Cowes, opting instead to continue to the head of the harbour area and into the wide River Medina. He was fairly confident that they had shaken off the hunters, at least to allow sufficient time for Nobby to get back to him in order to plan how they might bring Rahman to justice. But 'fairly confident' left room for a margin of error and he was trained to reduce such margins to a minimum.

He was hoping to find a mooring in a marina on the eastern side, a hope fulfilled when a gruff voice over the radio confirmed the availability of a mooring for their 32ft boat. He knew that there was a foot ferry here that could take them over to Cowes town centre if they wanted to buy some supplies and to eat there later on.

It was 8pm and quite dark as they secured the mooring lines and were sitting talking about the evening ahead over mugs of strong coffee.

John felt quite relaxed as he sat back in the cockpit and surveyed the Marina scene as its dozens of boats and their owners were settling down for the night. The light over the cockpits of some and the light shining from portholes in others that, along with the smells of cooking drifting across the water, were the more obvious indication of sailors preparing their on-board dinners.

'I think that we can give ourselves a night off tonight Janina' said John.

'There was no contact in Ramsgate, and I can't see how they can easily track us to Cowes.'

'Yes' agreed Janina 'And a place like this must have the best fish and chips and I am ready for a second go at that tasty British dish.'

After tidying up the boat - Janina had learnt that the phrase 'making it shipshape' was a sailing expression for keeping the boat tidy – they walked the short distance to the foot ferry. Following a short journey across a calm River Medina they made their way slowly along Cowes twisty High Street. An affluent clutter of mainly small shops most still open to take advantage of the late summer trade. Favouring restaurants, take-aways, chandleries, estate agents, and shops offering a variety of fashionable sailing clothes – Janina paused by a rack of tee shirts displayed outside one of the few more down-markets shops. White, red or blue shirts printed with: 'Captain' 'Crew' 'Cabin boy' 'Cook' and 'Dogsbody'. 'What's a dogsbody John?' 'Well, a dogsbody is the person on board a boat who gets to do all the jobs that nobody else wants to do'

'Sounds like that's the tee shirt I should have.' she laughed. 'I think that we should buy that one and also the Captain one in your size Janina. You might have started as a Dogsbody, but you seem to be picking up sailing skills at a rate that means you might well need the Captain's shirt before we finish our journey.'

Having completed their purchase, and bought some fresh fruit, bread, and milk, they found a restaurant specialising in seafood. They were led to a window seat looking out over the harbour with its range of bright lights...those of navigation buoys, moored boats, and of the few boats still moving in and out of the harbour.

Looking round Janina observed that: 'This does not seem much like the fish and chip van from where we bought fish and chips a few evenings ago John'.

'No, here we will be politely served with dishes of three times cooked chips instead of deep fried chips tipped in a bag, guacamole instead of mushy peas, and lightly battered fish with freshly made tartar sauce rather than heavily battered fish with the ubiquitous brown or tomato ketchup sauces, the former cod having been caught today and of the finest quality, the other was probably three day old second-rate fish. Oh, and no pickled onions here.'

After finishing her meal Janina suggested that both the basic and the more refined version of fish and chips were equally good as eaten in their different settings.'

'Right, it's only 9 o'clock, we need to find a decent pub so that you can learn that not all British pubs are like that dismal run-own pub we were in by the Yarmouth Yacht Station.'

It did not take them long to find 'The Anchor' in a narrow lane just off the high street. They were drawn into the pub by the inviting frontage and the live music coming from the main bar. 'This looks to be a pretty lively place.'

said John, as he pushed open the door. The bar was only about half full and at the further end was a small stage on which a band made up of middle-aged men were playing a Johnny Cash song.

They bought drinks at the bar and found a table in a relatively quiet corner of the bar. 'Well, I can now see the Johnny Cash connection' he said, pointing to a colourful poster on the wall above Janina's chair 'This band are called the 'Fulsome prisoners', they are billed as a Johnny Cash tribute band. So I guess we are in for an evening of music from a playbook originally written and sung by the 'Man in Black' – which suits me fine'

'I have never heard of this Johnny Cash' said Janina.

'But the music sounds nice to me and those guys are pretty good musicians'.

Just two numbers in, the door of the bar burst open and group of about sixteen, obviously fit, and by their suntans and brightly coloured shorts and tee shirts, obviously sailing, young people, poured into the pub.

Most went straight to the bar and stayed there, but five of them picked up their drinks and walked over to an area of the bar set aside for playing darts.

One of these came over to their table and addressing John, he said that they were trying to make up three pairs but only five of them wanted to play so did he fancy making up a pair. 'No thanks' said John 'But he did look at Janina 'What about you, do you want to learn how to play this traditional British pub game?'

At first Janina was reluctant, but the sailor was eager, indeed very eager, for her to join them. She gave in, shaking her hair free of her cap as she stood up. The tall sailor seemed keen to take responsibility for introducing her to the game. He informed the others that himself and Janina will be making up the third team.

While the game was going on John squeezed through to the bar and managed to catch the eye of a busy barmaid and buy another beer. Standing at the bar he asked an older member of the group why they were in Cowes.

'We are two crews of boats involved in the Little Britain Cup racing regatta here we have two crews of eight and we have recorded a first and second place today so we are celebrating with a few or more beers tonight.'

As he sat back down at their table John was looking at Janina and her new friends. She was laughing and did look really lovely, a beauty emphasised by her having gained a light tan from but two days sailing, a warmer colouring setting off her azure blue eyes. It was a loveliness not lost on most of the sailing group.

Goldie, Zerya, Jo, and Irvin had accepted that it had become too dark to carry on searching through the marinas. Goldie and Zerya were now going through the five sailing clubs located in the Cowes Harbour area. And Jo and Irvin, having been joined by Mick and Craig, were working their way along the High Street checking each restaurant and pub as they progressed.

By the time they arrived at The Anchor they all felt ready for a drink and so all four of them entered the pub.

John glanced up as they entered and he immediately froze, spotting straight away that these four stood out in their civilian combat type clothes. They might have been anglers in for a drink after fishing off the harbour wall or off the short pier. But something about the way the leading two moved made John think military. They might not be the thugs pursuing us he thought, but we have to assume they could be and so plan for the worst.

He watched them work their way to the bar not too gently pushing others aside as they went. Irvin was slightly taller than the noisy group gathered at the bar and John saw his gaze fall on Janina and him leaning slightly to talk to Jo who then followed his look towards her. He took a mobile phone out and unknown to John, called up a picture of Janina that the hunters had been provided with.

'Fuck, that's her' said Jo. 'I will call Goldie' 'No' said Irvin

'Look there are four of us, armed and ready, why wait for Goldie to claim the credit. We can get the job done......can you see anyone who might be her protector?'

'There is that bloke sitting at the table in the corner whose looking like he's enjoying the game of darts. He doesn't look that hard but I can't see any other candidates likely to feel our wrath.'

'Right, we can't pull the weapons out here so we will finish our drinks, leave and sit tight outside until they come out then we won't fuck about, once clear of the pub if it's quiet enough we will finish the guy off with the shotgun and grab the girl. You Craig, leave now and get the car....park up at this end of the lane by the waterfront. Once we have the girl I have a few ideas on how we can make her tell us where the boat is – a nice orderly gang rape will probably feature......afterall, either we will be disposing of her before we leave this poxy Island or we will be taking her to the boss for him to do the job. Either way she will be telling us where the goods are if she doesn't have them with her.'

Watching one of the four leave John was now sure that these were their pursuers. And although recent experience suggested they were probably armed, he calculated that they would not draw guns in such a crowded location...... The band had just begun their second set for the evening and were into 'Riders in the sky', as Janina was being escorted back to their table by her darts partner who she then introduced to John as Ben. Ben did not need a second invitation when John invited him to join them. Soon Ben and John were exchanging some sailing small talk and Janina went off to look for the toilet.

'Look Ben' said John 'We have a bit of a problem you and your friends might be able to help us with. Janina and I are sort of on the run. As you can see I am rather old for her and I don't have much going for me in the way of prospects. Her family of wealthy eastern European businessmen based in London are determined to prevent our marrying. They want to send her back to Lithuania to marry a second cousin.'

John was feeling a bit guilty at spinning this story, but he would later admit to enjoying getting into thinking up the details.

Ben was obviously disappointed to learn how close the couple were, but he was intrigued by the idea of a chase, especially one involving a fellow sailor. 'What were you thinking?'

John indicated the three men at the further end of the bar and asked Ben if he can get his friends to surround them and prevent them from leaving the pub for about 10 minutes to allow them time to get clear.

'I can't see that will be a problem.... give me five minutes to spread the word and when I give a signal that we are ready you can make your move.'

'Be careful Ben they might be armed. I can't see them using guns in the pub but just in case make sure that you guys press up close to them so they don't have room to draw weapons..... and step back if they do draw guns.'

'You seem to have gotten lucky John, at least three of the guys are army reservists and two of these for Special Forces, I think that they are going to enjoy taking the lead in this.'

When she came back to the table John indicated to Janina to get ready to leave while he observed Ben as he was quietly circulating amongst his friends. He saw the whole group move as one slowly down the bar laughing and joking as if in high spirits as they surrounded the three thugs. At Ben's signal, John and Janina made for the door and were soon out running along the dimly lit streets as they worked their way swiftly back to the ferry.

They were back on board the boat by midnight and John immediately set about making the boat ready to leave the Marina. 'I don't think they know where the boat is Janina, otherwise I think they would have staked it out and waited for us to return. It would have been much easier, less public, to take us here rather than in the busy town. But we will set off and motor out of Cowes.'

Although against navigation by-laws John thought it best not to turn on the boat's navigation lights until they were clear of the entrance to the harbour.... then it was red for port, green for starboard, and white at the top the mast. But even before he had time to do this the harbour masters office were on the radio pointing out his error. And they were also warned about a heavy storm, predicted at 10 and above on the Beaufort scale, due within the next 24 hours. Wind speeds that would cause all but the most foolhardy sailors to seek the comfort of a port. John reflected that it was unusual to receive a storm warning from a harbour master as it was assumed that any sailors would be up to date to weather patterns 'Hum.... must be a seriously strong storm gathering' thought John.

The short trip along the Solent went quite well, running on the engine rather than sailing due to a fairly strong head-wind and John's wish to get some distance between them and Cowes. He was thinking that he needed time to take stock and was hoping that Nobby would soon be getting back to him. Given the notoriously strong tidal stream that twice a day flows into the Solent from the west he decided to moor in the shelter of Hurst Point until the tide slackened. The Point is composed of a long strand of shingle that arcs out into the entrance to the Solent and on which sits Hurst Castle, another relict from the Napoleonic period.

By 7am they had managed to get a couple of hours sleep and were now resting in the cockpit eating a breakfast of fresh fruit followed by boiled eggs and toast washed down with mugs of milky coffee.

John noticed that Janina was wearing her new 'Dogsbody' tee shirt. 'I see that you are prepared for you role today Janina' he said smiling. 'Yes, all 'ship-shapeness' and ready to go captain' she replied adding a brisk salute.

She sat next to him and reflected on the previous evening.

'John I have been thinking about the story about us that you said you told to Ben.....about us being runaway lovers.'

'Well, I just thought such a tale would be easier to understand but I would admit to feeling a bit guilty at even that fairly innocent deception of such a nice guy.'

'Yes, but it wasn't so much the deception, it just made me think that you and I have spent four nights living closely together, neither of us has any emotional commitment to another partner, at least as far as I know with you. And yet you have not made any moves towards something more intimate. Do you not find me attractive, or perhaps you do have someone special in your life?'

He stretched out his legs, raising his head slightly to look beyond the headland in front of them to the green-gray sea beyond.

'Yes, I do find you very attractive Janina, who wouldn't, but there is someone special to me......not as a partner but as a daughter. Let me explain.....nineteen years ago I was in a relationship but it broke up partly over my often having to be overseas. She, Angela, was quite ambitious, working for a finance investment company in the City of London. The grumbling discontent with our occasional separation, and to be honest a more general difference in interests, built up to become something of a crisis during what was intended to be a romantic weekend in Paris. Suffice to say the relationship ended in a furious row when we were standing on the Pont des Arts Bridge overlooking the River Seine and, although we travelled back to England together, we then went our separate ways. Me back to Four Two Commando based just outside Plymouth, and Angela back to a flat in a block on Battersea Park Road.' He paused to take another drink of coffee and continued

'I had reluctantly but realistically accepted that the relationship was over and it was time to move on. But just a month later I received a letter from Angela informing me that she was six weeks into a pregnancy.

She did emphasise that there was no going back in terms of our relationship but that she intended going through with the pregnancy and felt that I had the right to know that I was going to be a father. I would admit to mixed emotions.....a tremendous sense of responsibility, but also a nervousness that for the first time in my life, at the still young age of twenty three, I had something, some deep emotional tie, that will be with me for the rest of my life.

In due course, the baby, Natalie, was born and my seeing her snuggled up in a cot at the Battersea flat about a week after the birth irreparably sealed the connection.'

Janina had become quite engrossed in John's outline of his experience but was finding it difficult to relate it to her original question about the two of them. Was he so hurt by the break-up with Angela to allow himself to become vulnerable again? But that was nineteen years ago, she was unsure.

John was at least partly reliving in his mind his earlier experience.

'So all went quite well for a couple of years with Angela being flexible about my having access when I was in the country. But when I went to Natalie's third birthday party there was another guy there, Mark, who was introduced to me by Angela as her new partner. It wasn't long after this that they were married and had moved to Berne in Switzerland for them both to pursue their rising careers in finance.

Contact was then reduced to occasional visits when I could get to Berne. But most of these visits, as nice as they were for me, generally only amounted to a walk in a local park with an ice cream and perhaps a meal in a cafe. Natalie was becoming more fluent in Swiss-German than English, so even our talking together was difficult. Angela had two more children and even the occasional visits were obviously unwanted and I did feel that I was causing Natalie more stress than happiness so I accepted the situation and tried to get on with my life. My relationship with my child became one of contact being based on our exchanging, first letters and then, as she moved into teenage years, it changed to e.mails.

Just after her eighteenth birthday she e.mailed to say that she was coming to England to study medicine at Cambridge

University and after her first year living in her college's hall of residence she was hoping to share a flat with some newly made friends.

We met up and within a few months of her being in England her spoken English had improved sufficiently to allow our conversation to flow more easily and our meeting-up became fun. Our relationship was much more obviously felt as being mutually supportive. My, by then, being in the Met. police and living in London made our meeting up easier because Cambridge is only about an hour's drive from London. And equally, London was only a short train ride from Cambridge, allowing Natalie to visit me and for us to take in a musical show, concert, or more serious play, in the west end.

But I am sure that you did not need to hear about all this stuff Janina and I am coming to your question about us'

'That's fine John. I have a sense that this was an experience that needed to be talked through and I am so happy that your relationship with Natalie has come good'

'Yes and the issue between us Janina is that I see you more as contemporary of my now nearly 20 year old daughter. I am twenty years older than you and when I saw you with Ben last night my negative view of our age difference was reinforced by how well the two of you looked together. I feel really protective towards you Janina, and emotionally I feel you more as a much younger sister, or even another daughter. I feel that we are going to stay together in some way but not as lovers.'

There was an extended pause before Janina reached out to him, taking his hand in both of hers.

'I do accept what you are saying John and I suspect that my feelings might have been more about a need for physical release after the pent up stress of the recent past....in fact now I think about it I really like the idea of having a big brother.....and if I ever meet up with Ben again I will be all over him big-time!'

'Take this', he said passing over a folded piece of paper – Ben wrote his e.mail address and phone number, and I am pretty sure that once we have sorted out our current situation he will be very pleased to hear from you.'

As Janina went below to clear up their breakfast dishes John's phone went off. 'Hi John, Nobby here......how are things with you, any recent contact?

'Well there has been contact but thanks to a bunch of local sailors we have eluded the bad guys.'

'So what's your plan now, where are you heading?'

'The plan is a bit fluid just now, I was hoping that you might have a suggestion meaning that we can stop running.....but if you need more time we will be heading west and I am thinking that we might make Plymouth. Mind you, if the weather deteriorates even further we might have to find shelter in somewhere such as Poole, Dartmouth or Salcombe. But a very strong onshore wind could see us having to ride out a storm at sea......anyway what progress have you been making?'

'I have had a meeting with the commissioner and she is very keen to collect a specialist team together but because she is aware of the extent of corruption within the Met she wants a bit of time to select a team of suitable, squeaky clean, officers..... It looks like we can definitely get down to Plymouth in the next few days and take you both to a safe house at about the same time as we exercise search warrants focused on Rahman's headquarters and also trigger the arrest of Rahman and the leading members of the organization here in London.'

'OK Nobby, meanwhile I don't want to hang around anywhere for too long, this bunch seem to have agents pretty much everywhere, even in heavy weather I think that it would be advisable for us to sail on.'

'I'll get back in touch when the team here is ready to go John.'

By mid-morning the tide had slackened and although there was now quite a sea swell and the wind had picked up, John decided to set off. He soon plotted a new course and sensibly decided to put a reef in the mainsail to reduce its sail area and to use just the smaller number 2 Jib. A combination of sails that should make the trip across Studland Bay and further west more comfortable. Or rather a bit less uncomfortable as they would be beating into quite a strong headwind.

As further preparation for the forecast bad weather he went over the boat making sure than all vents and hatches were closed, turned off the seacock to the sink and toilet, and made sure that any equipment on deck such as the life-raft was securely lashed down.

Janina did similar with the interior, making sure that all breakables were safely stowed away. John also insisted that they both wear harnesses and that these were clipped on to the safety lines running the length of the boat.

'Right, all set, let's raise anchor and get under way.'

The few days sailing they had experienced gave John the confidence that his sea sailing skills were returning and his natural disposition caused him to be excited at the prospect of a challenging sail west along the south coast. After manoeuvring to port to clear the head of Hurst Point he then bought the boat to starboard and headed past the multi-coloured sandy cliffs of Alum Bay then past the Needles lighthouse and the short row of standing rocks that lead out from the western end of the Isle of Wight. Within half an hour they were clear of the Solent and feeling the pressure of a force 7/8 wind. With a light drizzle in their faces and white foam whipping off the top of waves.

'This is properly good sailing.' Thought John, pulling in the tiller to harden up the sails, with the boat cutting through the waves as it heeled over on a port tack.

Later that day in Argyle Square the evening sun was going down as the square's primary activity was picking up, with girls and a few men in dimly lit rooms going about the business of satisfying eager punters. Many of these up from mundane lives in the suburbs for their monthly fix of young flesh.

In his office a pensive Ashif was sitting behind his desk contemplating the latest failed attempt to capture or kill John and Janina. It was so frustrating that what had previously been his most effective operatives had been unable to retrieve his goods and waste the troublesome pair.

He was thinking that couple of dickheads, Joe and Irvin, had not reckoned on the cleverness of the hunted pair, and had only belatedly made Goldie aware that they had spotted them. Now the four from London, and the two local agents, were having to trawl round all the possible mooring sites in Cowes to see if they can find them. We have repeatedly underestimated the Hardy guy. And it looks like they could well have already slipped quietly out of Cowes and sailed away.....where too being unknown.

A knock on the door interrupted his thoughts. Come in, he shouted, what the fuck do you......oh hi Bill, this is an unexpected visit.'

Bill leaned over the desk.

'Look Ashif I think that you have a problem related to information on your network of Met and some regional police contacts, and also some valuables.'

Ashif was relaxed about admitting to the embarrassing situation he was in. He had known Bill 'Nobby' Graveny for some time now and knew that he was the Met. officer who received the highest level of payment from the Organization, indeed his off-shore bank account in Antigua must easily amount to over a million pounds gained over the past few years......a nice retirement pot to be enjoyed when he left the force and was living full-time in the bungalow overlooking the sea that he owned via a shell company, nicely located on the southern side of that beautiful island in the Caribbean.

'So how did you get to hear about our recent difficulty?'

'Yesterday, about lunchtime, I received a phone call out of the blue from a John Hardy, a name I think you might be familiar with'

Ashif jumped up, pointing his finger at Bill

'How the fuck could you have heard from this arsehole....'

'This guy that you call an arsehole is in fact a pretty tough cookie Ashif. He and I worked together for about four years in the Serious Crime Squad during which we became quite friendly. At one point I was going to approach him to offer the opportunity to connect to your organization, but he always seemed so straight, never tiring from telling me how much he hated bent coopers. But look Ashif, I need to know if my name is in the notebook that you let them get away with.'

'Yes, it is there with all the others but my handwriting is not easy to read and if you remember, you first gave your name as William Graveny rather than Nobby and that has always been how your name has been recorded during our dealings. Presumably the John guy hasn't yet picked up on this.'

'Yet.... being the operative word' said Bill

'We need to get him ASAP.' It is fortunate that he trusts me and is expecting that at some point in the next few days I will be meeting him in Plymouth with a team of Met. officers to take them to a safe house.'

'Or rather' interrupted Ashif....'A team of gangsters we will temporarily second to a version of the Metropolitan Police, one composed of Goldie, Zerya, and some others who we are sure they have not seen before. We can even have a couple of our guys in uniform and use marked police vehicles, just to enhance our team's assumed identity..... If this John is convinced that you are straight Bill then presumably we can lift them from Plymouth, relieve him of the gun we know he has, and then take them to a supposed safe house, say somewhere up on Dartmoor. Then once there 'gently' persuade them to hand over the goods.'

Ashif was getting into the plan now, licking his fat lips and continuing......

'I am liking this plan, not least because it will allow me to personally finish the girl off and the killings will be carried out well away from anywhere public – nicely tidy.

Now I think about it, we do have another operation going on down that way dealing with some upstart gangsters trying to muscle in on the local drugs trade, so we already have additional operatives, led by Kurt, down there. And he assured me that he should have the local villains sorted within a few days.'

When Bill had left the office Ashif called Goldie and said for the group to catch the first available ferry back from the Island and get up to the office as soon as possible, as they now had reliable information on the couple's whereabouts, and a plan for an intervention that looked solid.

Chapter Four

At this time, while their boat was ploughing through the wind stirred waves in the unsettled section of sea off Portland Bill known as the Portland Race, an event was unfolding in the coastal city of Plymouth that would in due course come to interlink with their own circumstances. The city's police headquarters had just been alerted to a shooting in a more run-down part of the City, an area that, as yet, had passed by the gimlet eye of inner-city developers. Poorly lit streets lined by rows of terraced housing, with front doors opening directly onto the footpath. At a junction between two streets lay a young man who had just been shot once in the chest and three times in the stomach and was bleeding his life out as a passer-by was endeavouring to come to his aid, but a stream of his warm life-blood flowed steadily into the gutter.

The police radio call alerted a patrol car that had been cruising the area as part of an initiative intended to drive out or at least reduce the number of prostitutes operating in what is a residential area. A street-based body-selling activity working at the lowest end of a vice industry that was growing in the City. The end that was more about survival for mostly drug-addled women, and occasionally men, selling access to their bodies for day-to-day survival, and the next hit of cocaine, rather than much else.

The police car arrived on the scene to join an ambulance that was already there. Inspector Jean Boyd alighted from the front passenger seat of the police BMW and crossed over the narrow road to assess the situation. Two medics were by then bent over the young man and one of them looked up as Jean approached holding out her warrant card and asking for an update on the patient's condition. The senior medic stood up as her partner took over the attempt to staunch the flow of blood.

The two walked a few yards from the immediate scene and the medic shook her head.

'He has lost so much blood I think that shock will soon set in and that's almost certainly the end.'

'Do you think that I can talk with him just very briefly?'

'Well, to be honest I can't see that it would make much difference now but bear in mind that this could be the last few minutes of the lad's life, so let's not cause him further distress.'

After thanking the medic Jean walked back to the victim, kneeling behind him so that she was not interfering with the busy medics. Jean lent forward and speaking quietly into the boy's ear asked if he knew who had shot him. The boy slowly opened his eyes, eyes that were showing fear.

'...am I going to die?' he asked.

'Not if these medics have any say in the matter and if you really dig deep and fight to live.' said Jean

'Did you see the gunman?' The boy closed his eyes and his breathing was becoming shallower and he whispered the words....

'The Organisation, please tell Ross'

'Who is Ross?' asked Jean, but she could see that the boy was now unconscious.

'Right', said the leading medic. 'Let's get him to A. and E. ASAP and call ahead to let them know we are coming, and it will be on blues and twos all the way.'

As they wheeled the stretcher into the back of the ambulance Jean confirmed that it would be Derriford A. and E. where they were headed.

Looking down at the congealing pool of blood she noticed a couple of 'deal bags' in the kerb. It looks like cocaine she thought, and this was probably an aspect of why the shooting.

As she was travelling back to Crownhill, the Plymouth Police Headquarters, Jean was thinking about the young boy, now struggling for his life in the hospital. She had been aware that there had recently been evidence of some sort of low-level drug conflict going on in the region. But this was the first shooting.

Back at the station she bought a coffee and a ham salad sandwich from the self-service canteen, intending to eat this back in the open plan office she shared with colleagues. As she sat down the middle-aged officer occupying the desk next to hers looked up.

'Hi Jean, how is the vice sweep going?'

'Well, pretty standard procedure, more about us acting to deter potential punters than harassing the working girls. But we did get diverted to a shooting that gives cause for concern...... You are our lead on drugs Colin, have you heard of something called 'The 'Organization' or someone called Ross? She placed the two deal-bags on her desk.

'I can't think of a Ross in relation to the City's drug trade but The Organization is quite well known to drug squads across the whole country. We suspect this group is based in London and it seems to have no problem with obtaining a plentiful supply of marijuana and more especially of high quality cocaine. The word 'Organization' seems appropriate given that they have an extensive network of agents who themselves run teams of pushers working at the local level. This group have come to dominate the drugs trade in our region and, although tonight's shooting is the first recent drug-related use of guns in Plymouth, there have been two deaths by stabbing, and a few other non-fatal incidents. And there have been shootings in Exeter and Truro a year or two ago, with three deaths so far. We assumed this had been part of the Organization's activity when it was initially involved in the process of taking control. For the past couple of years the violence has been minimal. The word on the street is that The Organization dominates the trade due to fear of the violence that its agents have access to, and their willingness to use it. It is also thought that the Organization is involved with a range of other criminal activities – involuntary people trading to supply prostitution, prostitution itself and the related porn industry, a protection racket, contract killing, and more recently diamond smuggling. So pretty much a multi-product corporate concern.'

'Wow! that was quite a concise and informative briefing Colin – working in the drug squad sounds more exciting than the more mundane policing I am involved in.'

'It might be exciting but it is also quite depressing to see lives ruined by addiction.'

Having written up her brief report and up-loading it to the newly installed e-filing system of the Plymouth Police data-base she located her red MGB in the car-park and headed home to her modest cottage in the typical Dartmoor village of Peter Tavy about 8 miles north of Plymouth.

As she drove through the outer suburbs of the City she was reflecting on her life more generally and on the rather dismal state of her social life. Yes, there was the occasional game of tennis and she had been sailing with the Police Sailing Club. But these were activities mostly undertaken by couples and she had felt somewhat uncomfortable, being the odd one out. Still, I do have a career she thought, and if I can get involved with a significant initiative this must improve the prospects of further promotion. And of course, I have my lovely classic MG she thought as she flicked on the overdrive to ease pressure on the engine as she accelerated down the winding country road.

Six months earlier a young man had been planting some lettuce seed in a finely tilled seed-bed at the corner of an allotment site spread along the side of a low hill above Plymouth. The allotment was on a rare piece of open space at the edge of an extensive area of social housing. Housing built originally between the 1930s to the 1950s, intended to house the increasing number of people migrating to Plymouth to work in the naval and commercial dockyards and in the smaller manufacturing and service businesses growing in the City. But by 2010 the skilled, relatively higher paid jobs, had pretty much disappeared due to a combination of overseas competition and new technology displacing human jobs. Then, the post 2008 austerity had added to the demise of much of the decent work available. Since the Thatcher/Major promotion of neoliberal economic policy of the 1980s, continued during the subsequent fifteen years of the Blair/Brown New Labour project, the housing had become ever-more run down. When the dignity offered by having decent paid work goes many lose the motivation, and the money, to maintain homes and gardens. Most gardens today had broken down fencing, scrubby lawns, what had once been pretty flowerbeds were now choked with weeds, and in some broken down old cars were quietly rusting away. A few of the properties on the periphery of the estate were in private hands, most initially bought under the politically motivated rather than socially useful right-to-buy initiative. But then these being soon traded on to property investment companies whose owners aimed to maximise their investment by maximising rent levels. Few of those living on the estate were living in houses without some form of state income being necessary to support them, and support at the level of quite modest material lives.

For teenagers growing up on the estate life was generally spent on local streets with few prospects a decent job, and with many following elder brothers, cousins, or neighbours, into the army or navy. But for others the choice was mostly between only poor quality – fast food, care-homes, seasonal work, and similar - minimum waged work. Street lives for many was about cash in hand work usually on building sites, some petty theft, handling of stolen goods, or some modest marijuana growing and selling. All in an environment where violence or the threat of it, rather than the police, maintained what order there was.

To find a teenager working on an allotment was unusual to say the least. And one from the Plymstock estate was unique. But for this young man it had been a sanctuary from the more turbulent life on the estate. And the allotment also provided a break from the responsibility of being in effect a carer for his mum since he was 10 years old when her M.S.

became increasingly disabling. At first, at the age of about eight, it was simply curiosity that caused him to look over the low fence at the coming and goings on the site. But fairly soon he became more interested in an elderly allotment holder who began to say hello to him. Within a few weeks the old man, Tom, invited the boy to share his flask of tea and some biscuits. Within a few years they were working as something of a team, the boy doing most of the digging and hoeing and Tom organizing the planting.... what to plant, when, and where. He also retained responsibility for the weeding as he wasn't sure that the boy yet knew weeds from seedlings. The years went by and a close friendship developed between these two.

For the boy it was like having a wise granddad if one not shy about spreading his wisdom to the point of regular repetition. For the boy this predictability was part of the attraction of the friendship. On rainy days when they sought shelter in Tom's tool-shed he would teach the boy a little about the wildlife on the allotment – the foxes, hedgehogs, and the different types of bees and butterflies. He also learnt about some of the birdlife - that it was Goldfinches whose tinkling song and bright colours were a feature of many a spring or summer's day. They both enjoyed feeding the bold little robin that would take meal-worms from their hands. The older man also encouraged the boy to read, lending him books, including adventure stories such as 'Swiss Family Robinson' and 'Treasure Island'...then more descriptive novels by authors such as Charles Dickens, Thomas Hardy, George Elliot, and the boy particularly liked 'Les Miserables' by Victor Hugo. Tom had lit a fire that was to continue to burn as the boy read more and in doing so his gaining a more detailed sense of people's personalities, their social circumstances, and learning much more about the world beyond Plymouth.

It was now a year since Tom had died quite suddenly, suffering a heart attack whilst watering his much-loved runner beans plants.

The boy who had grown into a young man was distraught at losing his friend and mentor, but it was some compensation that Tom had often said that he would not want to linger on into a decrepit old age, and would rather die suddenly. The allotment management committee had long been aware of the friendship, indeed the boy had often helped some of older committee members with heavy work such as digging or carting manure.

So, a unanimous vote was cast in favour of the boy taking over Tom's allotment.

Today the young man who was planting the lettuce seed looked up as he heard his name called, it was his friend Harry walking up the path leading from the site's main gate.... 'Ross' he called again.

'Hi Harry, I thought we were all going to meet up on the Hoe later today.'

'Yes, we were, but I felt there was a development you should know about as soon as possible.'

They both sat on the seat in front of the shed.

'OK, so what's the issue?'

'Well Simmo has been stabbed and although he will recover, I think the conflict we were expecting is ramping up and we need to respond in kind.'

This conflict was an outcome of Ross and some of his close friends deciding to take on the Organization's control over the Plymouth drug trade.

It was Ross who had given the group a focus on mounting a direct challenge whereas the others, if frustrated with their lives, had been endeavouring to get through life by gaining a modest income with petty crime, odd jobs, along with some low key drug trading under the radar of the Organisation's local agents.

Ross had over the past few months gradually persuaded, perhaps more inspired, his three friends to join him in a challenge to the Organisation – not with the intention of taking over the local trade but instead to bring it to an end or at least reduce it to a minimum

Ross knew that he had become an idealist – taking on the might of the Organisation in order to free Plymouth from its evil grip, for better or worse his city. But of more relevance to him, to free people from the scourge of hard drugs.

He had seen too many ex-school friends and their families suffer the personal and social consequences of addiction, with at least four people he had known dying from an overdose. Indeed his friend Charlie and his brother were taken into care due to their single mother's addiction. And for Simmo it was the addiction of both parents that led to his also going into care.

What began for many a casual use of cannabis, was extended to the occasional fix of cocaine to brighten up boring times. But gradually, relentlessly, what had been a brief escape from a boring, unfulfilling, life had become a narrow focus on the next fix and in endeavouring to gain the money to fund the need.

It was a couple of months back when the four close friends – the four rather than three musketeers as the called themselves – had committed to a course of action that Ross had outlined. A friendship that had been sealed in blood. They were about 12 years old when they had gathered in the allotment shed as Harry led them through a sombre ritual of mingling a few drops of each of their blood together. Blood squeezed from small cuts on their wrists made with his penknife.

These four, had grown up together protecting each other's backs in school and on the estate.

Harry and Ross had experienced single parent families and Simmo and Charlie had spent almost all of their lives in care.

For Ross the four friends were part of the detritus of society, the rubbish left over as the wheels of capitalism turned. The class of people expected to work out the next 40 or 50 years in low paid jobs and to be grateful even for this. And this simply due to an accident of time and place of birth – some born into riches, most born into a life where their experience was of half-decent schools and of supportive parents. So at least the opportunity to make successful material live. Then, for Ross, there are the rest, constrained by circumstances to face a life of underachievement and poverty.

He had spent some time reflecting about his life and prospects.... supporting his mum and, in the absence of a father, feeling responsible for his two younger sisters. He did want money, not for flash cars or expensive trainers, these held little attraction for him. He wanted security for his family, for his close friends, and for himself. And the only realistic way of obtaining this was crime, and for teenagers such as him this mostly meant the drugs trade. But for Ross this was only part of the answer, he wanted money but he also wanted self-respect, and an idea was fermenting in his mind that might be a way to gain both.

He had come to hate most forms of authority – of those who hold coercive power over the lives of others. And for street life in Plymouth, and it seems the whole of Devon and Cornwall, criminal power was in the hands of the Organization. He slowly came to formulate a plan to seriously challenge the trade. He knew that this would require a ruthlessness that at least matched that of the Organization's agents. But he was expecting that his form of ruthlessness would be cleverly deployed rather than the crude forms of violence used when the Organization was crossed. He felt he knew the Organization's weak-point, its 'Achilles Heel', as he remembered about a leading character in a book 'The Iliad' given to him by Tom. The weakness was not the street-dealer or even the local agents that run them. Although these would come to be involved in any attempted challenge. But the key weak-point for Ross was in the supply chain for drugs and the return chain for the money gained from the sale of these.

Ross's friend and mentor Tom had also passed on his passion for at least trying to improve the world. For Tom it had been an ambition that had been at least partly fulfilled by decades of working as a Trades Union officer and being actively more politically involved as one of the few genuine socialists in the Labour Party. Even more practically his wish to help others had been slowly absorbed into years spent as a local councillor on Plymouth City Council. These were community level activities involving such work as advising on debt management, or trying to improve education provision, campaigning for more and better-quality social housing, and more adequate support for the elderly. But Tom had never lost his dream of a better, nuclear free, environmentally sustainable, economically fairer, world beyond just the local

Ross had a fairly clear idea of the magnitude of the task he was assuming – he had an image of Don Quixote, a character in another novel Tom had passed on, A book Ross found to be very funny in places but also inspiring as the knight, Quixote, mounted on his aged, bony, horse Rozinante, managed to misread one situation after another leading him into a series of misadventures. From which he often had to be extricated by his long-suffering servant Sancho Panza. Quixote tilted his blunt lance at impossible challenges, all in the service of the noble task of doing good. Ross saw that taking on the Organization would perhaps be impossible, but it would also be noble. And for Ross and the three friends he had inspired, it was better to fail at a noble cause than to ignore the evil festering on the streets of their city.

It seemed that the police of Devon and Cornwall could do little but seek to contain the drugs trade. Their focus was more on the related activities of the addicts seeking money for their habits. So addressing the symptoms of the problem not the root cause. At last, the lives of the four friends seemed to be infused with a sense of purpose – they, like Quixote, might just be hopelessly 'tilting at windmills'- but the idea made them feel truly alive.

It did not take much asking around for the four to identify the main agent covering Plymouth and to understand the arrangements for the street dealers he controlled for gaining marijuana and cocaine already sealed in deal bags and for feeding back the money gained - less his and their cut - to his own controller.

The local agent was responsible for parcelling out the drugs to the street-dealers and for transporting the income to his 'line-manager' who rented a neat house in a quiet suburb of Exeter. Drugs were delivered from a trading estate in Biggin Hill, in South-London, to a similar trading estate adjacent to Exeter Airport. Where they were weighed out, bagged up, and boxed, before being loaded into a van and being taken to four towns in Devon – Torbay, Plymouth, Barnstable and Exeter itself - and another four in Cornwall – Truro, Falmouth, Penzance and Newquay.

The initially modest income stream from the streets of Plymouth being swollen as it was joined by income streams from other cities and towns of the south-west. This becoming a veritable river of funds by the time they all flowed into Exeter, usually at least £200,000 per month.

Also sharing the Exeter house were two heavies whose role was enforcement and guarding the money gained up to the point of its being passed on to the London based link. A delivery that usually took place at Fleet Services on the M3, where income from the west county would be added to by similar amounts garnered from the southern counties – together amounting to up to about £500,000 cash per month.

Their role in the local enforcement of trade by the two heavies was usually swift and almost always violent, to the point where they had access to two handguns and two sawn-off shotguns. When not being used the firearms would be stored at a lock-up garage nearer the city centre. If more often brute force with sometimes an expertly wielded knife were sufficient to deter unwanted behaviours now that control had been established. This primarily coming to mean behaviours that threaten the Organization's monopoly of trade, be this up-start competitors or very occasionally their own agents foolish enough to engage in some unofficial freelance dealing.

It was Charlie that had used his old motorbike to follow the Plymouth agent to the Exeter house. An exercise he repeated for two more monthly trips. Following the most recent one of these trips, they assumed that the money would not be kept for long in Exeter. So Charlie and Ross then shared a stake out of the house for two days and nights. Whilst keeping their distance and using the well-worn bird-watching binoculars that Tom had past on to Ross. Then, early on the second day they saw an obviously hired transit van being loaded with a number of sacking bags and some builders tools.

'That must be the money heading to the next stage' said Ross

'I wonder if this trip will take us straight to London. If it does it will be interesting to see where the head-quarters of the Organization are located.'

The van left Exeter driven by one of the heavies wearing builder's overalls with the other in casual clothes following at a distance in a black ford fiesta. The two friends were cautious about tailing the van and car for an extended distance, thinking that they would risk being spotted. But Ross reasoned that if this was a monthly trip undertaken for at least the past three years since the Organization moved in then perhaps they might be less than vigilant. So they decided that they would follow the van and car for roughly 100 mile stretches. And, each month, two days after the delivery to Exeter, to wait at the previously noted 100 mile mark and follow for another 100 mile stretch. As the van was hired the graphics on the side were quite distinctive so it wasn't difficult to spot the van and the following black Fiesta. They were thinking that they were not in any particular hurry and in breaking down the tracking of the loot they would be less likely to be noticed.

It only took two such trips before they had followed the heavies to their liaison point at Fleet Services on the M3. The two men from Exeter were joined by two others from Brighton and two from London, the six just briefly exchanged greetings and fist-pumps before they were passing the sacking bags of money one way and then larger bags of drugs the other. The exchange took place in a quiet corner of the extensive car parking area and was completed within about ten minutes. The six then stood talking and smoking for a few minutes before the Exeter and Brighton vans left the car-park. The London heavies then took it in turns to use the Service's toilet and to buy coffee and sandwiches.

'That's when we will strike' thought Ross, 'When only one of them is with the van.'

Going back to the meeting at the allotment six months earlier...... once the two were comfortable in the sun-warmed seat by the side of the shed Ross reflected....'So Simmo, is the first casualty in a conflict that could become much worse before we smash the Organization's hold on Plymouth Harry.'

'Smash? That sounds like you are giving it large considering how small we are in comparison to what we are taking on.'

'Yea, but we have to be ambitious Harry, anyway, what's the extent of Simmo's injury and how did it happen?'

'Well, this is the story as he related it to me so allow for just a bit of exaggeration. He was down on Union Street in the early hours this morning trying to persuade a lad he knew quite well, believe it or not they were both in the Sea Scouts when they were young kids, to stop pushing hard drugs. He said that the lad was too frightened to stop dealing. These two were then approached by the local agent and the obviously scared lad started shouting for Simmo to fuck off and that he was enjoying his work. Then next minute the agent – that fucking lanky crop-haired bastard Carl Kimble, who we think is responsible for fatally stabbing that young kid in the dock area last month - who had two other street dealers with him - jumped on Simmo and threatened him with a blade. Stupid Simmo tried to grab the knife and as a result took one in the belly.

The arseholes run off, but fortunately door security at 'Jesters' came to his aid. These security guys now get first aid training which was useful given the amount of blood leaking from Simmo's belly. Anyway, an ambulance was called and he was cleaned up, stitched up, and back home in bed by five this morning. His sister texted me to let me know and I went straight round to see him and to find out what had happened. I think he was very lucky as the wound was just into the flesh and according to the Doc. down at the A.E. he should recover fine. And no doubt be his daft self again soon. When I saw him about an hour ago he was video gaming and licking his wounds. Mind you he is also intent on sorting the agent out...it's now personal for him.'

'It's personal for the four of us' said Ross

'But revenge will need to wait until we make the first serious move, which I think will be in a couple of months.'

On the next expected date for moving the money from Exeter Ross, Charlie, Harry, and Simmo, were parked up in the Fleet Services enjoying sausage rolls and coffee bought from the cafe. The car they used to get there was a VW Golf stolen the previous day by Harry and now running on false number plates. Simmo was driving as they felt he was not yet well enough to be involved in the more physical activity they were expecting to engage in very soon.

'How much dough do you think we will get?' asked Simmo.

'I hope it is enough for us to buy into or set up a legitimate business.....mind you, it would also be nice to have a new motor bike and some flash racing leathers and helmet'.

Harry piped up. 'I want to help mum buy her council house, and get her a new washing machine so she does not have to go down the laundry every two weeks'

'Let's not get beyond ourselves.' advised Charlie. 'We first have to do the business...... Funny but I was really nervous on the drive up but now I am looking forward to some action. One for all and all for one guys' He said as they then did a group high five.

It was a dry late June day and the car park was quite busy with travellers taking a break from the motorway routine.

As previously, the six tough looking operatives of the Organization arrived in pairs and each of their vehicles drew into the usual parking area. Fifteen minutes later the Exeter and Brighton vans had driven out of the Services heading south on the M3. Within a couple of minutes, the first London heavy headed into the Services main building and Ross walked casually up to the van and asked the remaining heavy if he knew the way to Heathrow Airport – He was abruptly told to fuck off, but the short distraction had drawn his attention from Harry and Charlie, who had been making their way behind the heavy. Harry stepped forward and hit him hard on the shoulder with a baseball bat. He sunk to his knees but was still conscious until Charlie hit him on the side of the head with an old fashioned cosh borrowed from an old lag living on the estate.

Ross and Harry jumped into the van while Charlie ran back to the Golf. The van sped out of the car-park just as the second heavy was coming out of the Services building. 'Brilliant' said Simmo.....'this is one for me being stabbed.'.... he drove over the foot of the heavy and smiled broadly when he heard the man's cries as they followed the van out onto the motorway.

They had soon turned off the M3 and were running west along the A303 – Passing the atmospheric ancient monument of Stonehenge, and the newly opened Haynes Classic Car centre. They pulled into the Cartgate Services and Tourist Information Centre and, after buying coffee and bacon rolls, they unloaded the bags of money into the Golf and, leaving the van in the Service area, they were soon back on the A303 heading towards Exeter and on to Plymouth via the M5 and A38.

It was late afternoon when they had parked in the little used car-park in the shadow of the Tamar Bridge. They quickly loaded the bags into the back of an old Vauxhall Astra that they had borrowed for a couple of days. They then left the Golf parked in the car-park, having planned for Harry and Charlie to return later that evening when the two of them would torch the Golf – no finger-prints and no DNA.

On the allotment Ross was able to drive the Astra close to his plot and he and Simmo unloaded the bags of money then stored them under in an already prepared pit covered by loose floorboards in the shed – there were only a few gardeners tending their allotments and Ross hoped that they would assume that the bags contained fertilizer, lime, or peat, for the plot.

'Right, put the heavy padlock on......let's get the Astra back and then catch the bus down to down to the Hoe to meet Harry and Charlie. They should be finishing with the Golf about now'

When, just after 10 o'clock, the four got together on the famous area of Plymouth known as the Hoe they were winding down with a few bottles of beer sitting on a grassy area overlooking the wide Plymouth Sound.

Historically the Hoe is supposed to have been the site of Francis Drake playing a game of bowls prior to his engaging with the Spanish Armada in 1588. As Tom had told Ross, the story is just another piece of nationalist mythology, half-truths archly re-presented as simplistic stories – he might have been playing bowls but it was unlikely that he would then have stepped straight onto a boat and set sail......and it is even less likely that he personally had much to do with the defeat of the Armada - the focus on him, whilst suiting the interests of the nation state for so called heroic figures, in effect erased the role of Lord Charles Howard and more especially of the thousands of sailors from England and a range of other nations who took part – Tom had suggested that the defeat of the Armada was due more to unfavourable weather conditions and the poor decision-making of the Spanish Admirals......... But in any case, the nationalistic version of Plymouth history meant very little to the gang of four, indeed to pretty much anyone in their generation and social class living in the city.

The four were stoked up with a sense of the immensity of what they had achieved that day. The money had been roughly counted and Ross gave them a figure of about £500,000.

'Wow,' said Simmo 'Let's get spending.'

'That's just what we mustn't do' replied Harry.

'We don't want to stand out, we need to see the reaction of the Organization. I think that they will be all over the cities in the west country – for sure they will be looking for whoever had the nerve to rob them and if we start buying flash clobber, watches, motorbikes or cars they will be down on us....in terms of spending we need to keep our heads down for at least a few months....mind you, if we stick to our original plan to upset the Organization's operation in Plymouth then we do have other work to do.'

'Well perhaps we can just have some pocket money to make our lives just a bit nicer,'

'I do like the idea of pocket money said Simmo.....I have never had pocket money, only heard about it as something most other kids got.'

'We all have to be involved in how we play this so how about if we take say £100 each week as spending money and reassess in a month or so?' suggested Ross, he went on to point out the next problem was how to launder the bulk of the money so that they could use more than small amounts.

'I don't think Plymouth Council will accept 100K in old banknotes for your and my mum's right-to-buy their Council houses Harry..... I have thought about this, and we don't have to rush – I suggest that we each open bank accounts with say four different banks and over the next year or so we will make two relatively small £200-£500 deposits each month – Amounts that will hopefully be below the surveillance level of the banks' deposit and withdrawal payment systems.

Over the past years, the other plot holders on the allotment site have become used to seeing the four of us hanging out on my plot, and we have always been pretty well-behaved and respectful so I don't see that we would have a problem with sharing out the monthly payments when we are up there. Even if we do meet two or three at a time rather than all four every month. I think that one of us should take responsibility for recording who gets what and when, just to ensure that the share out will seen to be fair.'

'You do that Ross, if anyone is the brains out of us four it's you.' Said Charlie 'agreed' echoed both Harry and Simmo.

As the evening drew on and each of the group had given their own generally exaggerated versions of their role in the day's action, they came to focus on the next one. Harry acknowledged that he had raised this a bit earlier but now suggested that they leave any specific planning for this to another day and just kick back and enjoy this evening.

'Let's finish the beers and head into Union Street for a kebab.'

It was two days later when the four had gathered at Harry's mum's house.

'Mum's at work at the Carehome and young Billy's at school, or at least I hope he is and not hopping off again, so we should have the house to ourselves for a few hours.'

In the kitchen they made coffee and toast using a brand new toaster that was Harry's first present to his mum. The next would be the washing machine that he had long wanted to buy for her. They settled down in the small living room with its worn settee and matching armchairs.

'Right' said Harry 'We have done them for dough, now we need to disrupt the supply of drugs.'

The three automatically looked at Ross, expecting any plan would best come from him.

'OK' he said 'First we need to think about the Organization's perspective...... for them a small gang of yobs have simply robbed them. Yes, they would be pissed off and I think they will consider changing their arrangements for the exchange of money and drugs'

'Mind you' interrupted Harry 'They might stick to the original arrangement in the hope that the gang would be stupid enough to strike again and they can then deal with them reinforced by some additional security'

'Yes, that's possible, but bear in mind that the Fleet Services is usually quite busy so a shoot-out or serious fight would quickly draw attention and probably the police'.

I think they will want to avoid anything too public and that they will probably relocate, which is fine as we will just track them down.......In due course we can go for the money again once we have at least disrupted the drug supply. For the time being, providing we can keep a low profile locally, I think that the initiative is with us.......Before we formulate a plan for our next move what is the word on the street about the Organization's response to last week action?'

Ross looked at Charlie because he now lived quite close to the city centre – once he had become too old to stay in care he had been placed in a one room bedsit in a decrepit old building located in a run-down area of the city.

'Not much so far' said Charlie. 'Other than Simmo and me being approached by a prominent street dealer yesterday, he asked us if we knew of anyone who might recently have come into money..... When I asked why he wanted to know this he said that he was only doing what he had been told to by his local supplier.'

'That's the least we could have expected' said Harry 'A low key search for us. I guess that the Organization doesn't want any weakness to be broadcast.'

'So far so OKish then' said Ross 'For our next step I suggest we go for the Unit on the trading estate by the airport where we know the drugs are delivered to on the way back from the exchange with the London heavies. They won't know that we are aware of their activities there' –

'Yes, whilst they probably can't understand how we found out about the Fleet Services meet up......they would not necessarily assume that the delivery to the Exeter airport unit is known' said Simmo.

Ross acknowledged this and suggested that they would still need to stake out the unit to ensure that the delivery arrangements continued as previously.

It was just a month later that, having confirmed that the activities at the unit suggested that it was still being used to process drugs, they were ready to go again.

This time they were wearing balaclavas and armed with two sawn-off shotguns Charlie had bought and collected from a local criminal fence come arms supplier with some of the money already taken from the Organization. As before they had a stolen car, this time an Audi A3, and on the drive up to Exeter they finalised who would do what.

Charlie and Harry had the shotguns and they would hold any security at bay while Ross collected up the drugs. Even though he had now fully recovered from the stabbing Simmo continued as driver due their having agreed he was the best fast driver.

It was early evening when they pulled into the trading estate, now fairly quiet as most of the units had closed for the day. They knew from their observation of the unit that about every hour or so two or three of the workers engaged in processing the cocaine and marijuana into deal bags came out for a smoke. It seemed funny to Simmo that the drugs den was a non-smoking area, presumably one of the trading estate's health and safety rules.

The unit was signed as being a delivery service as a cover for the more nefarious business being conducted there. The three crouched down behind the unit's wall out of sight of the front door but in the eye-line of Simmo, who was parked some distance away within sight of the door.

After about ten minutes, two workers came out for a smoke break. And once they had flicked their cigarette butts away they turned to go back into the unit. Simmo briefly flashed the car's sidelights and the three moved swiftly into the unit.

They were confronted with the strangest of scenes. A high-ceilinged space with a line of trestle tables down each side with plies of weed being processed on one line and cocaine on the other. Two heavies were stretched out in deck-chairs watching T.V. as Charlie and Harry came up behind them and Harry ordered them to stay where they were. The two started to rise but on seeing the two raiders were armed they stayed seated. The workers on the processing lines obediently laid down on the floor when Ross told them to.

He then got straight into stuffing, first the cocaine and then most of the weed, into the hessian sacks they had brought with them.

Simmo had pulled the car up to the Unit and was soon assisting Ross.

Within but ten minutes they had cleared the Unit of all but a small amount of weed left scattered about the floor. Charlie looked to Ross for a signal to go but as he turned the security guards rose from their chairs and came swiftly towards him. Taken by surprise, he fired the shot-gun and the nearest guard went down groaning and holding his stomach.....whilst the second one dived at Harry who stepped to one side and then struck the guard with the heavy barrel of the shotgun, knocking him unconscious.

The four piled into the Audi, removed the balaclavas, and were on the M5 heading to the A38 and what they felt as being the safety of the streets of Plymouth.

The following morning, when the four were gathered in Harry's living room the mood was more muted. There was more of a sense of the seriousness of the task they had set for themselves. A gun had been fired.

Ross spoke up first. 'Look, I think we should hit the Exeter house for the cash in a week or so's time'

Harry interrupted. 'But surely, as we have stolen their supply then presumably they won't have any drugs to sell, so no dough in Exeter'.

'I suspect that more drugs will be sent to the West Country ASAP Harry, but we can easily check that it is available on the streets next week and, if so, we can assume that the shortfall we created has been made up. They don't know that we are aware of the Exeter House and, although I accept that there will only be about half of the money we took at the Fleet Services raid, it should still be a substantial amount. After that we will lie low for say three months while we think again.'

'So far all we have done is to temporarily disrupt the drugs trade in Plymouth – I think that we can assume that once we hit the Exeter house they will relocate from both the house and the processing Unit'

Taking the house ten days later turned out to be a straight-forward exercise. They took turns to stake out the house from two days prior to the usual time of the liaison with the London operatives. And on the expected day the hired van was driven up to the house.

The previous arrangement was repeated with Simmo driving, Harry and Charlie armed, and with Ross guiding the raid.

As the first heavy carried two bags to the van Harry and Charlie stepped forward and Charlie shouted for him to stand still. At the front door the second heavy was just coming out and Harry turned and pointed the gun at his stomach. It seemed that the previous encounter when one of their colleagues had been shot had somewhat reduced the will to fight of the heavies.

After this third successful raid the four were pleased to see that they had added another £250,000 to the treasure chest hidden under the floor of the allotment shed and now also had a sack full of cocaine wedged in between the shed's narrow rafters, their having dumped the weed on the Hoe for all comers to share for free.

It was a week later, following his being shot, that Charlie was carried into the A and E department of Derrifield Hospital. The ambulance crew were not that optimistic about his chances of surviving the shooting. Although the bullets seem to have missed vital organs, there had been a massive loss of blood. Mind you they were hopeful that as the victim was young and looked pretty fit there was still a chance.

Charlie was quickly wheeled into a cubical, lifted from the gurney to a bed and the leading medic briefly then read the handover to the consultant and her team. Nurses were already wiring Charlie to the various monitoring machines – at the completion of the handover the trauma team moved into a practiced routine skilfully choreographed by the consultant.

Three days later when the first police traffic officer was leaving the Plymouth police headquarters he found to his surprise a package by the door. This was taken to the reception where the Duty Sergeant opened the package to find a letter and what he was certain would prove by the colour and texture to be a large amount of cocaine. By the time the station's senior officer, Assistant Chief Constable, Peter Morris, arrived at work the package and the letter had been placed on his desk.

The message in the unsigned letter was fairly short, highlighting the insidious advance of drug pushing, and associated addiction, in the West Country and more especially in the City itself. And going on to challenge the police to take more effective action.

The package had been left outside the police station in the early hours by Ross. The decision to do so had been a result of his having been to see Charlie in hospital the previous day. Seeing one of his very best friends so close to death had made him even more determined to do all he could to disrupt the business of the Organization. It would need guns now he was thinking so a need to upgrade their firepower beyond a couple of old shotguns. He did have a nagging doubt about using the same shady source of guns as they had bought the shotguns from. He had been trying to work out how the Organisation's agents had tracked Charlie down.

At the hospital Charlie had whispered to him the words one of the two gunmen had used just before they each shot him.

'You will not steal any more money or goods from us you bastard.'

Charlie had survived the attack, due mainly to the skill of the medics but also to his determination to survive. The more obvious link was that Charlie had been the one of the four friends to meet the gunsmith, 'Jake the Peg', and complete the transaction for the shotguns.

The Organization's agents could quite easily have tapped into local street knowledge to locate Jake, and Ross doubted that it would have taken much to persuade him to finger Charlie as a lad from the estate. As Charlie had been identified the link to his three friends could soon follow, mind you, this might be delayed due to the local community not being too open with outsiders. 'We do need to think about taking some precautions, and the sooner we can get some modern guns the better.' Thought Ross.

Ross's hunch about how Charlie had been identified was pretty accurate.

Kurt had left the senior management meeting in Argyle Square two weeks previously with the Koch pistol in his overnight bag and a growing anger in his head towards the gang that was endeavouring to screw the Organization's operation in the Southwest. He had always taken a particular pride in the smoothness of the operation in areas under his control and no upstart pissing bunch of pretend gangsters were going to upset this. He had come too far up the income and status ladder from petty crime and door security, protection, and drugs....... in all of which his career had been provided with uplift due to a love of inflicting hurt, allied to an at least workable understanding of human psychology, so how to invoke obedience if possible, but also fear when necessary.

So far, the feedback from operatives in Plymouth, Exeter, Penzance, Torquay, or indeed any other city or town in Devon or Cornwall of any competition with street-level drug pushers, was just of minor issues with a couple of sellers being mugged. And, as yet, there haven't been any sign of any local yobs appearing to have suddenly come into money.

Within six hours he had collected two shotguns, another Koch pistol, and two hand grenades from the Park Royal unit.

'That Benny is a miserable nob-head' He thought.

'But then I suppose that cleaning and maintaining various types of weapon for most of the day while also having to attend to the main business of importing massive tubs of kebab meat does not seem to be all that exciting.'

He was thinking that requesting two hand grenades was a clever addition – If he did catch all four of these pricks in a flat or house at the same time then one grenade lobed amongst them, if messy, should do the trick, and save on expensive ammunition!

By the early evening he was pulling into the driveway of the new house in Exeter where the regional operatives had been ordered to re-locate too. Still in a nice quite suburban area, if one a bit nearer to the City's Cathedral.

Kurt had phoned ahead to ensure that the two heavies based at the house, and the two from the Unit that had now been relocated from the airport industrial estate, would be present, along with Carl Kimble the regional boss. And he also expected that the double order of chicken wings and chips he had told Carl to get delivered would be there.

As he entered the living room he was pleased to note that the four heavies immediately sat up strait and greeted him with appropriate deference.

'You dickheads make it look more like an A and E dept. in here. With all the bandages and the leg splint.'

'Yea, these gangsters took us by surprise' said the fattest heavy, 'But we are all recovering quite well and ready to take these guys down, just say the word Kurt.'

'Well, the word is pricks for you sorry lot – The boss is not happy and if he is not happy then we, or more precisely you, should be very careful. We, or rather you, have fucked up – fortunately the Organization's drugs-base and other income streams are flowing quite well across the rest of the country. So this issue here in the South West is seen as more a little local difficulty rather than a more serious problem....... Mind you, this also makes you lot stand out as a failing group – get it!'

A mixture of energetic nods and yeses made Kurt feel that he had made the point.

At the police headquarters in Plymouth Peter stood up and walked over to the window overlooking the City while he tried to absorb the message in the letter. He had been aware of the increasing drugs-related crimes but he and his boss, the Chief Constable, were continually having to balance resources available with public and political pressures.

For Peter, the primary policing difficulty was in cutting the supply of drugs at source – his local experience suggested that there was little point simply continuing to apply the current strategy of arresting or harassing the street level pushers or their controllers. We need some alternative strategy that can identify the supply chain and try to cut it off at source.

He was thinking that they do seem to have been avoiding recognising the significant uplift in the scourge of drug-taking in the West Country and perhaps this latest act can trigger an adequate response. If I am to persuade the Chief Constable that a change of strategy is not only necessary but can be effective then I need to undertake some finer grained analysis...... having thought about this during the morning he was beginning to formulate a way forward and an aspect of this being that he thought he could identify a local officer who might be able to help with this.

He picked up his phone and asked his secretary to arrange for Inspector Jean Boyd to get to his office as soon as possible.

Jean was sitting at her desk eating a bowl of canteen soup with a crusty roll for her lunch when her phone rang and she was informed that the Assistant Chief Constable wanted to see her is his office ASAP.

Goodness thought Jean. 'What have I done. I have never had such a call to the top floor of the building.'

She quickly finished her lunch, smoothed down her blouse and skirt and ran a brush through her hair. She also called into the toilet before getting to the ACCs office. She was soon perched nervously on a chair in the ACC's outer office when the secretary's intercom buzzed and she was told that he was ready to see Inspector Boyd.

Peter was behind his impressive if cluttered desk and he indicated for Jean to take a seat opposite. He could see that she was nervous.

'Please relax Jean, I have asked you to come up because I am trying to make the case for us to come down heavily on the West Country drugs trade and I would appreciate your becoming involved. Although the information I have been getting from other police areas suggests that we might be dealing with a national issue and so perhaps some national criminal body.'

He then set out an overview of the five-year pattern of drug usage.... focusing on statistics of arrests, overdose hospital admissions and deaths, and crimes such as burglary and shoplifting, which are traditionally associated with the need to raise money for drugs.

'As you can see Jean there has been a progressive and significant increase in all these indicators over the past five years.'

She was aware of an increase but had not realised just how much these crimes had been mounting.

The ACC continued. 'The most obvious conclusion from these figures Jean is that our current drug control strategy is not very effective. Indeed, whenever we have a serious blitz on community-level trading and supply those targeted always seem to have been alerted in advance, and so very little is achieved. Each coordinated bust usually just achieves about twenty arrests for personal possession and very low –level dealing, and results in up to half a dozen front doors being smashed down at properties where we had very good quality intelligence that they were supply and control centres. But that when we undertake comprehensive drug-dog aided searches they turn out to be clean.'

'Can I just mention something related to your information please sir?' The ACC invited Jean to continue, and she reminded him about the shooting that had taken place a couple of days earlier and how Colin, Sergeant Pardue, of the local drug squad had briefed her about something called the Organization that appears to be running the drugs trade in the West Country and possibly across the whole of Britain.'

'Yes we do keep hearing about some major criminal organization being locally very active. Indeed, the London Met. Commissioner thinks that she knows who heads it – but, as yet, they lack sufficient evidence to start making arrests. It seems that, similar to our own experience, they also have a problem with 'tip offs' whenever they try to move against these serious villains. Frankly Jean, in both London and here we are talking about police corruption!......

She also suggests that the illegal activities of this organization go well beyond just drugs – with prostitution and related people trafficking, protection rackets, and some more recent involvement in the blood diamond trade – so quite a crime-sheet. Our own Chief Constable will be liaising with very senior officers at the Met. primarily in terms of exchanging intelligence. He paused and walked over to the window. Spreading his arms out wide he said.

'Look Jean, that's the centre of our patch. About 500,000 people living in the City. Men, women, and children whose lives are being degraded by the increasing criminality we are experiencing, and I am determined to at least try to do more to stop this.'

He sat back down at his desk and, leaning forward he told Jean of his intention to compile a plan of action to be submitted to the Chief Constable for approval. And that one aspect of the plan will be for her to lead a team of carefully vetted officers to identify the drug supply chain as far back along to its source as possible. Hopefully much further from the local streets that our traditional short-term anti-drug initiatives have focused on'

'What are you working on just now Jean?'

'Well since I moved here from Dundee a year ago I have been a sort of spare inspector, and in the last six months I have been involved with an initiative to reduce pick-pocketing then more recently the anti-prostitution sweeps targeting punters rather than the girls in the city centre. But this draws to an end next week.'

'That's useful, so no-one in the building will be suspicious if you are seconded to another unit.....I really don't like to admit this Jean but we must have at least a few corrupt officers working in this building.'

'A new unit, that sounds intriguing sir'

The ACC placed an A4 notepad at an angle on the desk where they could both view it and pointing his index finger at the first open page he said.

'That is a diagrammatic representation of the structure of the new unit, with you taking the lead'

Jean immediately noticed that she had been noted as having the rank of Chief Inspector on the diagram.

'There is a rank error there sir, I am just an Inspector.'

'Ah yes, well units with the remit and staffing that this one will have would normally be led by an officer of the rank of Chief Inspector or above, so you will be holding the temporary rank of C.I. If the unit is deemed to be a success, then no guarantees, but I will do what I can to have the higher rank confirmed.

The unit will not be based here but in a building down by the Tamar that we closed as a working police station some years ago but fortunately have not yet sold on. It will be refurbished, at least to be minimally comfortable for a team of about eight. You will be leading the newly established 'Immigration Intelligence Unit' (IIC). A cover for the real drugs-related work, and hopefully one that any officer in the pay of this Organization will not see anything of interest in for their paymasters.

I know that they do have some connection with people trafficking but this is individuals brought into the country on false pretences – e.g. girls led into thinking they might working in the media or even as fashion models, but then forced into prostitution or pornography. So not directly related to immigration-related crimes.'

Jean sat back in her chair trying to absorb the implications of what had happened to her in but the last 30 minutes. From thinking she might be facing something related to a disciplinary to now being seconded to a significant initiative....in addition, looking at possible promotion.

'Here is a copy of my draft plan Jean, take a few days off, work at home and think about my initial plans for the unit. Then we can meet again at the end of the week and share ideas before I compile a final report for the Chief Constable.

But we must maintain the utmost secrecy. Even selecting untainted officers to join the unit will be a challenge. Sad to think that this is necessary but recent experience suggests that we have to ensure the security of this operation.'

For the next few days Jean would become increasingly engrossed with the idea of how the new unit could work. It would be bringing together her enthusiasm for policing in a general sense with her particular dislike of organized crime, especially when it involves drugs. The next few mornings were spent with an intense focus on staffing the new unit and on the detail of how it might operate. And in the afternoons she would drive up to Burrator Reservoir on Dartmoor and either fast-walk or jog round the large elongated lake holding water to supply Plymouth. This would allow a more reflective approach to the morning's more detailed focus, and so offer a chance to gain a clearer understanding of potential issues.

Whenever she was experiencing the steady rhythm of exercise aspects of her personal life would invariably intrude into her thoughts. Yes, it did seem that her career was going well but emotionally she still bore the scars of the breakup of her relationship with Duncan, the fellow police officer based in Dundee with whom she had spent two years sharing a flat and their lives. And although the parting was amicable, each had come to realise that they had quite separate interests outside of work, she had still felt the need to leave Dundee and begin a new life elsewhere.

But her mum, in regular phone calls from Dundee, did repeatedly remind her of her advancing years

'You are nearly middle-aged Jeanie, and our Sandra already has two bairns.'

Being reminded of her younger sister's happy family circumstances and fertility did not do much to convince Jean of some urgent need for her to breed, but it did highlight the lack of any meaningful relationship. Still, she reflected. '....even as an aged spinster I will have my career as well as a nephew and niece to spoil, and of course I have my little MGB!'

And it was the MG that she got back into for an enhancing drive back over the winding roads of the open moorland to her cottage in Peter Tavy.

At the end of the week she was back in the office of the ACC and together with Peter and her colleague, Colin Pardue, they firmed up the broader strategy, identified the mid to longer-term aims, and set out the operational details of the new unit in a report to go before the Chief Constable.
After Colin had returned to the main office the ACC and Jean turned to consider the staffing of the new
unit, not in terms of numbers and rank levels....as they had already set these as herself, an additional sergeant as well as Colin, four detectives constables from the Territorial Policing Unit and two officers from the regional Armed Response Unit. Now they had to consider how to select officers untainted by any possible hint of corruption.

'Part of the reason I have selected you to lead Jean, apart from your proven ability, was that you are still quite new to the division, so very unlikely that you would have established any connections to this collection of very unsavoury villains. As to Colin, I have worked with him for over 20 years – we were both promoted to be sergeants in the same month back in the early 1990s - and I would rely on my experience, allied to my instinct, so he was the second name I put down.

The next step is for Colin and yourself to get together and work through the service records and for you to combine this with instinct, and hopefully you will be able to identify seven untainted police officers. Given that we have over 3,500 full time police officers covering Devon and Cornwall, then if we can't even do this we might just as well all take our pensions and retire to the bloody seaside.'

Over the following week Jean supervised the move to the new Unit's offices, and with Colin's help had selected the admin. and policing staff to undertake the work.

Although she had been very busy it was during this time that she had been thinking about the young man shot two weeks previously, a shooting that was almost certainly connected to the local drugs trade. In attempting to track down the 'Ross' mentioned by the victim, Colin had been talking with his now ex-colleagues in the drug squad and with his street level snouts but the identity of 'Ross' continued to elude them.

Jean called the hospital to see what had happened to the young man, thinking that the answer would probably be that he had not survived. So she was relieved to hear from the ward manager, who she eventually got through too, that the victim, named she said, Charlie Greenwood, had survived. And although still in the hospital in Moorgate Ward, they were expecting to send him home in the next week or so once specialised home nursing and general care support had been organised.

The following day Jean called into the hospital on her way to the office. Near the entrance she was able to buy a couple of bars of chocolate at the Friends of Derriford Hospital shop. Once she had found the ward and having made contact with the ward manager and shown her warrant card, it did not take long for her to be taken to Charlie's bed. He was sitting in a comfortable chair beside the bed playing a video game on his phone. He looked up and smiled at Jean...

'What painful procedure are you going to put me through now Doc?'

I am not a doctor Charlie, I am Chief Inspector Jean Boyd from the local police.'

'Blimey a Chief Inspector.... this must be a special visit. I assume that the chocolate's for me, so thanks. But I can tell you straight away that I did not see and do not know who shot me, and I don't know why. I think it must have been a case of mistaken identity.'

'OK Charlie, I do understand your reluctance to point the finger but on the night you were shot you told me that it was The Organization and that I should let someone called 'Ross' know, do you remember?'

'So it was you who knelt down beside me that night....perhaps I was already a bit delirious.'

'No Charlie, I don't think that you were delirious, and I also think that I now know quite a bit more about the Organization. That they are a nasty bunch of London-based villains causing problems for young people like you and your friends throughout the south-west of the country.'

As Jean was talking Charlie was remembering the night he was shot and how comforted he had been by the encouraging words she had said about the determination of the medics to keep him alive. He knew that it gave him hope when he had been on the point of giving in to his fate....his outlook had changed from frightened despair, to a determination to fight to survive.

He decided to trust her and to judge how far he should open up depending on her reaction. He told her of the lack of confidence he and his friends had that the police can't do anything to halt the relentless advance of the Organization.

'A problem we have is that we suspect that the Organization actually has useful contacts within the local police force – bent coppers - and that makes us wary about passing on information.'

'Yes, I can understand your comments about the local police Charlie, but the most senior officers in the Devon and Cornwall constabulary are now serious about addressing the scourge of the drugs trade. I can't go into detail about any strategy we might have if we are going to take this forward, but I would say that whatever information you can give me will I am sure assist our aims, and it will be treated in complete confidence. It could also ensure that you get justice for the injuries that you have suffered.......Why did you have two deal bags of cocaine on you the night you were shot Charlie?'

'Well, as usual when we are out and about in town we try to interfere with street-trading if any opportunity arises. We carry balaclava masks just for that reason. Those two bags were from a bigger bag of about 20 deals that we had just taken off a street-dealer. I had emptied most of the bags into waste bins along the river path but I wanted to keep two of the smaller bags as we were going to test the quality.'

'Goodness, you do seem to be on a mission, so someone else was with you when you were shot.'

'No, my friend had already headed home as he had a call from his mum, she is disabled and he supports her.'

'You seem to have been viewed as a thorn in the side of Organization. Can you tell me a bit more about your friend and what your aims are?'

'To be honest I just want to get out of here and back to normal life but if you give me a contact number I will have a think about coming back to you.'

'That's fine' said Jean passing over her contact details –

'Call me anytime day or night. Before I go, I noticed that just now you spoke of 'we's' in relation to how the Organization and the local police are viewed. So I assume that you have been discussing this with a number of friends. Would one of them be called Ross? Can I have a chat with him?'

'Best left for now Chief Inspector and let me think about your comments.'

'OK Charlie, and it's Jean, by the way.'

Chapter Five

When Ross got home from visiting Charlie he looked into the living room just to see how his mum was, and if she wanted anything to eat.

'No I'am fine dear, but we have received a letter from my brother Tommy who, as you know, lives in Australia, that I want to have a chat about.'

Having made them both a mug of tea Ross sat on a low stool beside his mum's armchair. She unfolded the letter and passed it to him.

'As you can see, Tommy has been looking into our family history. There has never been much interest in this sort of stuff in our family, we have tended to live for today, so his letter came as a bit of a surprise. He says that his new found enthusiasm has have been sparked by a workmate who has a keen interest in something called 'genealogy'...anyway you have a read through the letter dear.'

At first Ross was reading the letter more to humour his mum than due to any real interest in family history, but the more he read the more he was drawn into all these names on paper, seemingly part of his family heritage, or at least their genetic and social heritage rather than a heritage of material good fortune.

The diagram that Tommy had compiled had Ross's and his sisters names along the bottom and alongside this Tommy's two children. Then above these Tommy and Ross's mum then above these his four grandparents – three of these were dead and the fourth one, granny Margaret, was living in sheltered accommodation just by the Barbican area of the city.

It was the names above these – the unknown individuals or new information about his grandparents that he had not known that began to interest Ross. His mum's dad serving in the Marines and a note of his being on active service in a place called Aden. A great granddad noted by Tommy as having served in the 8th Army in North Africa and Italy during World War II, and having been awarded the military medal. His great, great, granddad, noted as being killed in the Battle of the Somme in World War I. And an eighth-generation back granddad who seems to have been born in 1810 recorded as living in Plymouth, serving as a Marine...... stuck beside his name Tommy had attached a copy of a news-paper clipping.

The clipping outlined the work of a British naval unit called the West Africa Squadron. It seems that the ships in this group were tasked with enforcing the 1807 parliamentary act banning the trade in slaves – with a particular focus on the Atlantic trade. The unit operated between 1807 -1860, and the article stated that during this time the Squadron captured 1,600 ships endeavouring to break the conditions of the Act – releasing 150,000 slaves at the cost of the lives of 2,000 British sailors. And it seems that Ross's ancestor had been a Marine serving on HMS Solebay, one of the Squadron's ships.

'Wow,' whispered Ross to himself. 'That is really something to make you proud.'

His new-found interest in genealogy might be limited to his own family but he was hooked on the idea of learning more about the silent, seeming ghost-like, figures populating the history of his family's past.

In order to follow up this new interest Ross decided to visit some of the places noted in Tommy's letter – As well as the Marine connection he also wanted to follow up an intriguing detail noted in the letter about the place of birth of a generations-back grandparent born in 1840. This distant relative had been born in a place called the 'Workhouse' in Liskeard.

Having Googled 'Liskeard Workhouse' he learnt more about the institutions that seem to have provided very basic accommodation for the poorest of the poor. At that time it was administered by a Board of Guardians as a part of the

Liskeard Poor Law Union. He read of its being a meagre form of quite basic shelter provided at the cost of personal dignity for the victims of the workhouse system.

A report compiled at the time by the British Medical Journal was critical of the medical care available at the Liskeard Workhouse, and this only judged as relative to other workhouses. He read that the workhouse system had been developed from the Poor Law Act of the Elizabethan period – intended to provide minimal support for the unemployed, the disabled, the elderly poor, and single mothers. Presumably for Ross's relative, Jane Adcock, it was in this last category that her mother was consigned to the workhouse.

Inmates were expected to work for their keep, whether this be cleaning the workhouse building itself, working in its laundry for women, stone-breaking for able bodied men, or for both sexes the messy job of picking oakum for hours each day.

Husbands were separated from wives. Even minor breaches of the rules were harshly punished. Dignity was removed on entry to the establishment, with personal clothes being replaced by a uniform to mark the inmates out as just that 'inmates' of a 'charitable' institution – a marker of shameful poverty. No pension, sick pay, social housing or other type of benefit for the poorest in the 19th century only the degradation, and loss of personal freedom, of the workhouse.

Two days later Ross borrowed Charlie's old blue Honda 250cc motor bike and was crossing the Tamar Bridge into Cornwall then on the A38 towards Liskeard. About five miles before the town he turned right onto the country lane leading to the village of Menheniot, which seems to have been the home village of the Adcocks. He drove up a hill into this relatively small Cornish village of mostly gray slate-roofed, stone houses.

The first more substantial buildings he saw were the Church of St Lalluwy and St Antonious and the newer red-bricked Menheniot Methodist Chapel –

'So no shortage of religious enthusiasm even in such a small place' he thought.

It was a village of narrow lanes and fairly nondescript buildings. A general Spar shop/post office, and just further up a narrow lane from this the White Hart pub offering daily roasts and flagging up a skittles competition due to be held on the coming Saturday with 'all welcome'.

Ross had learnt something of the village's history from a Google search and he had read of a long history of slate quarrying, and of a shorter 1843-1870s boom in lead mining. He had also called up the 1841 census records for the village had seen quite a few 'Adcocks'. One listed as a tailor, another as a farmer, and two men and one woman were listed as servants.

It was the women, Sarah, that was of particular interest because her age of 30 suggested that she might well be the Sarah Adcock that a year later gave birth in the Liskeard Workhouse.

The coincidence of single motherhood and employment as a servant made a connection for Ross, as he remembered seeing a T.V. drama about life in big country house where the master's son had regularly taken advantage of the more attractive female servants. Then denying any responsibility for the more obvious outcome, with the unfortunate woman being sacked and sent home in disgrace. Perhaps this had happened to Sarah, and her family had either been ashamed of her in an oppressively religious village or could not afford to keep her and a child in what were, for most working class families of the time, very tight financial circumstances.

He walked around the small graveyard adjoining the parish Church and within the shade of a gnarled if still bushy yew tree he found a grave shared by three Adcocks with an invitation he could just make out for them to 'Find eternal rest with God' chiselled into the modest gravestone.

Leaving the church yard by the lynch-gate, Ross walked slowly round the centre of the village trying to imagine what it must have been like to live here over 150 years previously.

He was thinking that his relatives must have walked along these narrow streets, perhaps used the pub, and were christened and knelt to pray in the church.

'Although I would like to think that more of them had been members of the more independent Methodist congregation.' He said under his breath.

Following his eating a pub lunch, Ross was back on the bike and heading toward Liskeard by the early afternoon. He arrived just as a slight drizzle was starting to fall. After parking his bike in the extensive old market area in the centre of the town that now doubled as a car-park his first task was to find the site of the old workhouse.

He saw a sign for a library come tourist information centre and thought that someone there would perhaps be able to point him in the right direction. The cheery young librarian was more than happy to help - it was as if every day someone called into the library seeking out the location of the workhouse.

She guided Ross out of the library building walked them both about 50 yards up the hill and, looking to the left along the main road running through the town, she pointed.

'It's about three quarters of a mile down this road on the right hand side......most of it has been demolished but the old office and front reception buildings are still there, and there is a plaque providing some information on the building's sad history. There are two single-storied, white-painted, buildings......I don't think that you will miss them.'

It only took about ten minutes for Ross to walk the length of the high road, a road still just about retaining some older small shops including, a bakers, a greengrocers, a butchers, an ironmongers, and even a small bookshop, but these were retail survivalists, tenaciously hanging on between the estate agents, fast–food outlets, and invariably the charity shops, that together dominated the small-shop retail sector in the town, with two chain supermarkets dominating the larger shop business.

Standing in front of the remaining workhouse buildings all he could actually see was two examples of quite pleasant

Victorian architecture set behind a neatly trimmed lawn, lined on three sides with flower-filled borders. But in his mind's eye he could see the large featureless and dreary brick buildings that had stood behind and would have overlooked what now remained.

Whilst looking at the building he remembered the words he had read of the curriculum of the children's quite limited education....they were to be taught basic reading, writing, and arithmetic, and '...the principles of the Christian religion'.

It occurred to Ross that perhaps the local and national politicians could have done with reforming the Poor Laws in line with what he understood as the principles of Christianity, or at least of the primary founding inspiration of that religion. And failing this, then perhaps the local Board of Guardians could have been more Christian in their management of the workhouse itself.

The continuing drizzle and his imagination prompted Ross to think of the baby born into the depressing circumstances of the Workhouse in 1840, growing up on this very site. Her mother probably having been rejected by her family, now finding herself at the very bottom of society. The baby, named he knew as Jane, would have grown up being made aware on a daily basis that she was of the poor.....he could feel his fists clenching as he reflected on the unfairness of life in a grossly economically unequal society. Some born into wealth and privilege, others, such as Jane, born into poverty, which of these being determined simply by an accident of birth, set in the economic and social conditions that applied at that time.

As he was thinking back 120 years he made a connection between Sarah and Jane and the 2010 circumstances of himself, his friends, and almost all of the children and young people from the Plymton estate.

'We might have much better material conditions but we are fully aware of our being at the bottom of society, with few prospects for realistic advance. In this sense we share a level of despair that would surely have been similar to the outlook for Sarah and Jane. And yet over a century on I am here because of them......and I am trying to ensure that my generation of our family can be freed from the cycle of economic poverty and lack of opportunity.'

As he turned away from the building, and began his walk back up the high street, Ross felt quite embarrassed as he wiped away the tears that expressed the deep emotions that the experience of the Workhouse had stirred within him.

He had intended to call into Stonehouse Marine Barracks on the way home but such was the impact of the experience of Menheniot and Liskeard that he wanted a day or so to absorb this before he began to consider the military side of his family's past by following up Jane's marriage to a young Marine named John in 1860. A ceremony that, thanks to Uncle Tommy's research, he now knew had taken place in the Marine's Chapel at the Stonehouse base.

It was two days later when Ross decided to walk the mile or so from the estate to the Barracks situated by the River Tamar on the other side of the City. He wanted to continue to absorb his family's past and his own circumstances, and the City itself was a big part of this. The route he took was through the old part of the City known as the Barbican – He stopped to look at a colourful notice board that he thought he must have passed-by dozens of times without stopping to read. The board noted how in 1620 the ship the Mayflower left the quay with a group of Plymouth Brethren on board setting off to undertake the difficult passage to America.

It noted how 53 of the Brethren survived to reach the 'New World' and with the help of the Wampanoag native American tribe they were progressively able to establish a farming-based community. Without the support of the Wampanoag the group would have either starved or frozen to death in the first winter. At the end of 1621 the pilgrims and the tribe together celebrated the community's first harvest – an event that gave rise to the annual holiday celebration of 'Thanksgiving'.

As he walked on Ross reflected that their subsequent treatment suggested that the native peoples had little to celebrate given how the greed for land of settlers that followed the pilgrims effectively led to the end of their way of life as their and their fellow native peoples lands were relentlessly stolen by the invaders.

Ross walked up the hill past the Royal Citadel and on to the Hoe itself. From where he could look out over the wide expanse of Plymouth Sound. A stretch of water that had played an integral part in British history. Not just the centuries-long activity of the Royal Navy, but also the even longer history of the local fishing fleet that helped to provide the food for the people of the City.

He knew he cared about the City, at least the areas he knew best and people he lived amongst. And in the last few days he was becoming more aware of a deeper connection with his family's past and their close involvement with Plymouth. But to a significant extent he knew this was an involvement with the military – more especially the Royal Marines. He had felt that the royal title expressed a connection to one of the most significant wrongs in the country linking the Marines to a family of individuals with no intrinsic merit that were being economically supported and socially elevated above all other people.

The Queen herself had over the years acquired almost holy status. As if a large section of the British people were mesmerised into more or less worshiping this, in itself quite troubled, family. Rather oddly, he thought, in our meek forelock-touching way, we name public hospitals and schools after these people when they themselves would never use the NHS or the state education system, much preferring the more privileged private sectors of each.

In his two decades of life he had never heard the Queen speak up on behalf of the poorest people living in the lands she at least nominally ruled.

The military itself had always been a problem for Ross.....in Plymouth it had traditionally served as a way of avoiding unemployment or of working in low paid, low status jobs.....who would rather serve in McDonalds when they could serve in the Navy or an Army unit. But why do young men commit to an organization that sends them overseas to kill other young men they have never met and for the most part have never done them any harm – wars are usually started by elderly politicians, but they are fought by young men.

But his feelings about the military were becoming mixed. His recently learning about British sailors and marines working to stop the slave trade made him proud of his distant relative. And he also remembered old Tom talking to him about a unit called the Blue Helmets. A unit composed of soldiers from various nations grouped together under the command of the United Nations, deployed to conflict hot-spots and tasked to stand between warring factions and to protect civilians....known as 'peacekeepers'. And of course, there have been quite a few disasters – floods, hurricanes, tsunamis, earthquakes – when the discipline and resources of the military have been of real value.

'Why is life so complicated when you look below the surface' thought Ross.

His walk had taken him to the Stonehouse Barracks, today the base of 3 Royal Marine Commando Brigade. Walking around the group of grey-stone, obviously military, buildings in the part of Stonehouse where the public are allowed, he was thinking about the ordered ranks of men that must have marched from the Barracks to boats waiting to take them to lands across the world.....often leaving loved ones for months, even years, at a time.

He went into the austere building housing the Royal Marine Chapel, the location where he now knew the marriage had taken place between John Fletcher and Jane Adcock back in 1860 when they were both 20 years old. He was standing on the spot where two young people had come together and from whom developed the Fletcher line leading down to him... Ross Fletcher, now also 20 years old.

These last few days had given Ross quite a bit to think about in relation to his family and also perhaps about his own future. But he was also thinking about the next step in the action against the Organization.

Just a bit further up the Tamar from Stonehouse Jean Boyd was in her office with Colin and Tom, the two sergeants seconded to the new drug-unit, as together they had their first meeting to collate and analyse the intelligence their officers had been able to gain.

'So far' said Colin 'We have gained only fairly minimal information from the street-level sources. It seems that there is a considerable level of fear of whoever is organising Plymouth-based distribution. And we have similar feedback from the officers who have been focusing on Truro, Penzance, Falmouth, Newquay in Cornwall and Exeter, Torquay, Brixham, in Devon.

What has come through is that there has been some disruption of supply recently, which was presumably related to the 5 kilo package left outside Crownhill police station. But there seems to have been other issues related to distribution that we don't yet know much about. I am thinking that a challenge to the Organisation's monopoly of trade has caused a ripple of surprise that has reached the streets, if with much reduced strength.'

'How far has tracking the chain of supply and return of income reached?' asked Jean

'So far, our staffing focus has been on collecting and collating the intelligence we have just covered so the tracking of the chain up from street pushers has taken pretty much a back seat. But we have identified six very busy street sellers: two in Plymouth, two in Exeter, and one each in Penzance and Torquay, and the next step is to concentrate on shadowing these six on a 24/7 basis to see where this leads.'

Within half an hour of Charlie being released from hospital Ross, Simmo, and Harry were sitting with him in his bedsit sharing a veritable heap of MacDonald's burgers and chips much of this being smothered in tomato ketchup.

'That tastes really good' said Charlie – 'I think I am even skinner after three weeks in Derriford.'

'I expect that a week or so on a Macdonald's high carb diet will soon sort that out.....but in the meantime what was it you wanted to tell us about the local coppers?'

'Look Ross, and you other two, what I am going to say might sound odd given our view of Plymouth police and the drugs trade, and what looks like their accommodation, or at least tolerance, of it.

While I was in Derriford a women copper – a Chief Inspector Jean Boyd – paid a visit, she wanted to know if I knew who had shot me and why, and that she was sure it was connected to the drug trade. I had already met her on the night I was shot and, if it was the medics that actually saved my life, it was the words she whispered in my ear about hanging on and fighting to survive that gave me the determination to live....... she mentioned a new strategy for tackling the drugs trade and was aware of the Organization....it seems that she has been liaising with the London police'

'Hang on' said Harry 'How do you know that she's not bent. And just trying to find out how much we know?'

'To be honest Harry I don't, but where do we go from here? The Organization is no doubt still looking for you three......We do know that their local agents have been asking around and if they were able to finger me then it won't take too much to link the four of us....it is well-known on the estate that we hang around together.'

Ross looked up...'Yes, I have been thinking about this and we are vulnerable...we don't have the fire- or man-power to take on the Organization at its roots, which are presumably buried somewhere within the criminal underworld in London. All the time it is able to operate we will be targets – we have shown that they can be challenged.......they need to show any such threats to their operation will be rapidly and violently dealt with.....So, on balance, I think we should at least talk with this Jean Boyd.'

Using the phone number that Jean had given to him, Charlie phoned her to set up a meeting – she suggested the new office but he insisted that they meet in a cafe in the fairly isolated village of Princetown up on Dartmoor. And the next day all four, again having borrowed the old Vauxhall Astra, travelled the winding single-lane roads across the wind-blown moor.

It was just Charlie and Ross who walked into the cafe to meet Jean. They were immediately put on their guard when they saw that she had a male companion.

Having ordered coffee, they sat at Jean's table by the window and Jean led on the introductions. Charlie expressed their concern about the male introduced as Sergeant Pardue, or Colin.

'Colin here has spent the last two years since moving down from the Met. being frustrated at the lack of resources allocated to tackle the drug trade in the Southwest, and also by his suspicion that those running the trade are being tipped off when his unit try's to move against the operatives......He had left the Met. just because he saw the amount of corruption that was an obvious feature of the London force.'

'Yes,' said Colin. 'But from what I have heard from clean ex-colleagues in the Met. the new Commissioner and some of her senior officers are endeavouring to clean up policing in London. But it is very difficult to identify the bent from the straight coppers. Here in Jean's new unit, I do feel that I am now working with a clean team made up of staff dedicated to challenging the trade in this region.'

Ross interrupted. 'You talk about 'Jean's new unit', an internet search of Devon and Cornwall police does highlight the setting up of a unit led by Chief Inspector Boyd, but it states this as being the 'Immigration, Intelligence Unit'..... so how is this related to the local drug trade?'

'Look Ross' said Jean 'Can we leave the work of the unit until we get to know each other, we need to share what we know as we build trust between us.'

'Fair enough said Ross, do you mind if we ask two friends to join us'

This was fine with Jean and Colin as they already knew about the four friends due to their having had Charlie followed when he left hospital, and noting how often the four met up in even just the last two days.

Once having added two chairs to their table and ordering more coffee, they, now joined by Simmo and Harry, settled to continue their meeting.

Jean began again

'Look, I will be direct....were you the gang that we know have been disrupting the Organization's work in the South West? And did you leave the 5 kilos of cocaine at Crownhill?'

The gang exchanged glances.....and after a brief pause they shared almost imperceptible nods.

'That's, two pretty frank questions Jean' said Harry. 'What if we say that for now let's assume yes for the first question and yes for the second, just as a working assumption. And see where you want to take this'

'Firstly well done.....few people would have the guts to take on this criminal organisation ...you lot are like the Biblical David taking on Goliath. Can you explain why you decided on this very risky course of actions?'

Ross explained that. 'On the 'assumption''...... that they had carried out the actions just noted, it would have been because they had seen the gradual impact that the drug trade had had on degrading the community in which they had grown up. Especially the suicides and disengagement from social life of many of their school friends and other neighbours. It had been an additional element, along with un- and under- employment, and the poverty of opportunity and of hope, that was impacting harshly on the people of the Plymton estate.

Then, when the local agent stabbed Simmo we decided to act.

'Mind you' interrupted Simmo. 'We have also made money for ourselves during our actions.'

'I am not interested in the money, and let's face it you can't really thieve off thieves.....But can you explain how far back up the supply chain you reached and how you managed this.' said Jean.

Harry took the lead in setting out their tracking the chain from the street to their controller, Carl Kimble, then to the Exeter house and the drug processing and distribution unit by the airport trading estate.

He explained that, judging by the amount, it was pretty obvious that the money collected at the house in the Exeter was income, not just from Plymouth, but from various cities and large towns of the southwest region.

With some pride, he highlighted the strategy of tracking the money by stages as it moved from Exeter to the liaison point at Fleet Services.

After passing over the money and receiving the next load of drugs they assumed that the funds would then be taken to London. Harry then sat back and smiled at his fellow gang members ....they had enjoyed hearing Harry's outline, in an odd sort of way it was satisfying to show the professionals how it should be done.

'Well respect for you guys' said Colin. 'The meet-up at Fleet seems to have been a monthly exchange.... so 5 kilos of cocaine per month at a street value of about £500K. We are looking at £6m per year and how many regions is the UK separated into?

I would not be surprised if we were looking at something like £50-£75m per year. OK there would be fairly substantial costs of staffing the organisation and no doubt paying for bent coppers, but that still leaves a considerable sum for the man, or men, at the top. Perhaps of more interest.... this level of income represents sales of about up to 750 kilos of cocaine per year.... how on earth can they manage to import that amount of white stuff?'

'Yes, and from what intelligence we do have about the Organization' said Jean. 'If the most profitable income stream is drugs, this is only one source of income along with some other types of criminal activities .....Can we leave it there for the time being as there is quite a bit for us to absorb before we take the next step. But I want us to part by my reinforcing what Colin said earlier about the respect we have for you guys and I promise complete anonymity for you – only Colin and myself will know your identity. And I also promise that I will share with you the general plan, if not the operational detail, of how we decide to take this forward.'

Ross made the observation that: 'Although you have not explained how something named the 'Immigration Intelligence Unit' is so involved in tackling the drug trade I think we can assume this name is being used so that bent local coopers are not alerted to a new threat to their paymaster's operations.'

'No comment' said Jean 'Which means that you could be right, but I can't say!'

The group broke up and Jean and Colin drove back over a now mist-shrouded moorland landscape. They were fired up after hearing from the gang the way they had taken on the Organization, especially in the tracking of the supply-payment route from the streets of Plymouth to the liaison with the London thugs.

Jean reflected on what they now knew and on what to do next.

'The criminals would by now have relocated the Exeter house, the processing unit, and no doubt would have rearranged the liaison at a different location to Fleet Services. But we have Carl Kimble as our first link. I will run our plan before the ACC tomorrow so he can OK our intention of not making any arrests as we move along the chain, even though we know that the operatives are involved in ongoing criminal activity. To delay charging them, at least until we trace the chain of evil back to the Organization's boss.'

As Jean's MG was making its way back to Plymouth, Kurt was driving back to London musing on the past couple of weeks, during most of which he had spent re-organizing the Organization's West Country operations.

The shooting of the young lad gave him some pleasure and making Carl also fire two shots was useful in that he was now blooded, moving up from stabbing to shooting, and he should now find is easier to shoot anyone posing a threat.

It was quite clever he thought to think about the shotguns the gang had used and for him to have them traced to that dick Jake the Peg as the likely local provider. Who, when grabbed by the balls, quite willingly gave the lad, Charlie's, name and offered a rough idea of where he lived. Once identified it was like hunting a deer – careful stalking, then trapping him in that shitty street, then aim and fire! The comfortable weight of the gun and the controlled kick of the shots. A satisfactory result and although it was remiss of me not to check he was dead, I can't see that skinny young prick surviving four direct hits.

He had also taken the opportunity to give the West Country operatives a kick up the arse. The Exeter house had already been relocated and he had now organized the move of the processing unit to another trading estate, this time a much larger one, with the more secure coded entry access, on the northern outskirts of the city.

He had delayed his return to London just to make sure that the first delivery of income and the collection of drugs went smoothly. He could now leave the country hicks to themselves and head back to his natural habitat in the club and pub haunts of the London criminal underground.

Chapter Six

If we step back three weeks to the night that Charlie was shot, we find John and Janina aboard 'Sunrise' ploughing its way through a heavy sea. A force 7-8 headwind had allowed only slow progress as they were having to short tack their way west. Moving around below decks was possible only by holding on to the cabin sides and the fixed furniture and although heating soup was possible due to the gimballed gas rings, anything more substantial would have to wait until the weather eased. Looking up through the cabin hatch Janina could see a wind-blown John, dressed in oilskins, tightly griping the tiller, and although gritting his teeth he still seemed to be enjoying the sailing on the edge experience.

John had further reduced the sail area in order to make the boat more manageable, but he still preferred to steer by hand rather than rely on the more fragile autopilot. He was reflecting that it probably wasn't such as a great idea to sail directly though the turbulent Portland Race, with the normally rough conditions being made even rougher by the increasingly stormy weather that was rapidly closing in. But it was certainly exciting.

He was reflecting on his good fortune to have a boat sharing arrangement with his friend Chris. A seasoned sailor who kept his boat very well maintained, with all the fixed and running rigging, and safety equipment, in excellent condition, so important when tackling heavy seas.

Janina joined him on deck offering a welcome mug of hot soup. He could see that she was uneasy as she looked out over the high rolling white crested waves.

He reached out and gently touched her arm...'Don't worry about the weather, this boat is strongly built and models like it have seen worse weather than this – we are in about a Force 8 wind now and the sea will ease when we have passed through the Portland Race. If the weather does deteriorate further, with wind Force 11 or above, we will reduce sail even more and head for a port, such as Teignmouth or Exmouth, to find shelter until the weather clears.'

He checked Janina's safety harness was secure and set his gaze on the wave disturbed horizon. Two hours of heavy sailing later they were 10 miles on from the Race but the wind-speed had increased to the point where John lashed the tiller to leeward and went forward to hank on a storm jib and to reef the mainsail by another slab. This operation was only accomplished with some difficulty given that the conditions now included driving rain and cold sea-spray to add to the high winds. Even though they were still making steady headway John decided to head for Exmouth, the nearest sheltered port.

They were on the new course for only about half-hour when the radio crackled into life on Channel 16 – 'Mayday, Mayday, Mayday' sailing yacht 'Morning Cloud' with two adults and one child on board. We have a broken mast and one injured crew member, on passage from Santander to Brittany.... over.'

John waited to see who would reply and within two minutes he heard the Plymouth coastguard responding to the Mayday distress call. 'Receiving you 'Morning Cloud'.....do you have an EPIRB [Emergency, Position, Indicator, Radio, Beacon] if so, please turn it on, otherwise can you provide your current longitude and latitude position....over'.

'Apologies Plymouth coastguard... I am a bit stressed. I have now activated the EPIRB so you should be able to locate us. I would roughly calculate the we are approx. 80 miles off the south coast ....we are shipping water and the bilge pumps are struggling to cope....over'

'Calling 'Morning Cloud'... What is the condition of the injured crew member...over' 'Morning Cloud' calling Plymouth coastguard... I think it is a broken arm, quite a bit of pain, but coping for now...over.'

'Calling 'Morning Cloud'......I will get back to you as soon as I can assess which is the nearest available life-boat station. We are receiving numerous calls just now so please be patient.'

Whilst they completed the exchange of messages John had lashed the tiller again and had gone below to the navigation table in order to calculate the relative positions of 'Morning Cloud' and 'Sunrise'.

'Hm, I hope that the coast guard can identify an available lifeboat as I don't think 'Morning Cloud' will survive for long in these conditions, with those problems – the failing bilge pump could get serious and if the broken mast is dragging overboard then the boat could be turned beam on to the wind...not good.'

Within five minutes the Plymouth coast-guard was back transmitting to the distressed yacht. 'Plymouth coastguard calling 'Morning Cloud'..over'

'Morning Cloud receiving call...'

'Morning Cloud', all lifeboats suitable for these sea conditions and the distance to you are currently on call....I will now transmit an all boat alert to see if there is any boat that can get you soon...I would advise that you prepare to launch your life-raft'

John called the coastguard using the same Channel 16. 'Calling Plymouth coastguard....this is yacht 'Sunrise' on passage from Cowes to Plymouth. I calculate we are about 70 miles from 'Morning Cloud's' last position, so it would take about seven hours to reach her in these conditions....would be happy to try....over.'

'Plymouth coast guard to 'Sunrise' the conditions are rapidly deteriorating.....I cannot advise you to try for a rescue even if you are a very competent sailor, and that your boat is built to stand these conditions......our recent weather forecast indicates that the wind will be increasing to Force 12, so waves to 12 metres, and very poor visibility – I would strongly advise that you make for port, we do not want two distressed boats. These conditions are now becoming impossible even for the largest of boats.....Plymouth

Coastguard station is very reluctantly advising you to immediately seek shelter...over.'

'Sunrise to Plymouth coast-guard.....I very much appreciate your caution, but shelter not an option, and am changing course to head towards 'Morning Cloud's' last position. Please can you assist by keeping me informed as their position changes...over.'

'Plymouth coastguard to 'Sunrise'....I hope that you realize what you are taking on, bravery can be foolish – yes we will update every 15 minutes – God speed Sunrise!...over and out.'

'Well, as I am atheist, the God speed means little but I can appreciate the sentiment' Thought John, as he set course south-east towards the stricken boat.

For the next eight hours John was supported in taking occasional breaks from the tiller by Janina, with each of them taking turns to make hot drinks to go with the numerous biscuits they were able to eat. John was surprised and pleased at the way Janina just got on with helping to sail the boat. I do remember thinking of her as a lady in distress when we first met, but now I see her very much an equal in terms of determination and grittiness. I am an experienced sailor, but she is not, which makes her non-complaining willingness even more admirable.

'Sunrise' was being tossed up and down as she tried to cut through the swollen waves, but she only really rose up the face of each wave and then pitched down the other side. Regular calls from the coastguard allowed John to adjust course to keep heading directly towards 'Morning Cloud', and also updating him on the boat and its occupant's condition.

It was becoming quite dark when John assessed they were within half a mile of 'Morning Cloud' and he called the coastguard to ask her captain to fire two flares.

Five minutes later Janina pointed off the front port side – 'Fireworks!... over there.' she shouted. 'We call them flares at sea but fireworks will do.' said John as he pulled the tiller towards his body in order to steer towards the flare trails.

'Sunrise calling Plymouth coastguard... can I please have direct contact with 'Morning Cloud' to enable me to get close enough to take them off...over'

Plymouth coastguard to 'Sunrise'... please go ahead and discuss your positioning with 'Morning Cloud'...we are monitoring your exchanges, good luck, over and out'

As he was closing on the badly listing yacht John could see that she was very low in the water and her rolling motion suggested that it would not take many big waves to swamp her. He decided that the best way to complete a rescue was to get the crew of 'Morning Cloud' to launch their life-raft and they would then pick them up from this. After passing this request to the captain of 'Morning Cloud' – Richard – he took a long length of rope from a cabin locker under the cockpit seating and handed the tiller to Janina with an instruction to keep head to wind. He started the engine which, although pretty useless in a gale, he judged that it should help to maintain the boat's position during the attempted rescue.

He then went forward but it took him about 15 minutes to completely lower the main-sail and set the much smaller Try-sail. He then carefully made his way to the bow. Janina could just about make him out as he was sent up and down as if on a see-saw with the movement of the boat. John saw that the life-raft had been launched and was now fully inflated if still attached to the boat by a thick cord. He could see first a woman with her arm in a sling get gingerly into the life-raft, then a young girl of about eight was past down to her.

Before the captain joined them, he stood to catch the rope that John threw – as they had arranged. It took three attempts to throw and retrieve the rope in the strong wind before it was caught and had been secured to the life-raft. With Richard on board, John wound the rope round the starboard winch and steadily, if with some difficulty, pulled the bright yellow raft toward 'Sunrise'.

But before he started taking the crew on board he went back to 'Sunrise's' cockpit and, taking the tiller, he turned the boat downwind and, although this meant that the boat immediately picked up speed, the try-sail did allow for more sideways stability than would have been the case if the main-sail had been kept on.

John indicated for Richard to get on board first, this then allowed him to hold the life-raft stable while John first lifted the child off and then helped the women onto 'Sunrise'. All three were soon sitting in the main cabin, wrapped in heavy blankets and drinking mugs of hot soup.

'I really can't thank you two enough said Richard, we were in real trouble.'

'We are not safe yet' said John leaning in from the cockpit...'this strong wind will be blowing us all the way to Plymouth even though I have set a drog to slow us down.

John called the Plymouth coastguard to update them on the situation. While Janina comforted the child, Daisy, and administered paracetamol to her mum Sue.

As they approached Plymouth, John opened the VHF radio Channel 14 and called up the Cattewater Harbour Commissioner's the official body whose primary role was to oversee the running of the range of marine facilities covering the extensive port area of Plymouth. He received an immediate response to his request for permission to enter the harbour.

'Harbour Commissioner's Office calling 'Sunrise' – we have been kept informed of your recent action by the Coast-Guard and too bloody right you can enter the harbour, it will be an honour for us to have you with us......Please proceed to moor in the Mayflower Marina where an ambulance is waiting to take those rescued to Derriford Hospital for a standard check-over and to attend to what we have been informed is a suspected broken arm – good job sailor!'

John steered the boat past Drake's Island in the Sound, entered the Marina and, under the direction of the Harbour Master he was guided to the quay side where about a hundred people, plus an ambulance were waiting.

'Shit' thought John

'We are supposed to be on the run and in hiding, now it looks like we have gotten caught up in quite a public show.'

He told Janina to put a cap on and to make sure that her hair was concealed under it. He also got her to wear heavy sailing overalls so that she was quite shapeless. He was thinking that she was more likely to stand out than himself.

After seeing Richard, Sue, and their daughter, off in the ambulance, and receiving much backslapping congratulations from the fellow sailors that had gathered on the quay, John motored 'Sunrise' round to their appointed place in the Marina.

'I think we should relax for a few days Janina, then I will phone Nobby to see if he has put the team of Serious Crime Squad officers together.'

The next morning the pair were relaxing in the cockpit enjoying coffee and biscuits as they soaked up the late summer sun of a much calmer day when a figure came walking along the decking of the mooring, stopping by 'Sunrise'.

'Hi there' said the cheerful woman

'I am from the local on-line news outlet 'Plymouth Live', and would like to take a picture and interview you about your recent sea-rescue. I have already interviewed Richard and Sue of the Compton family and they were naturally very effusive in praise of your combined calmness, bravery, and undoubted sailing skill'

John was very wary about this request, but Janina seemed keen to talk about the adventurous 48 hours they had just experienced. John was thinking that it would only be a few days now and Nobby, and the crack Met. unit he was putting together, should be taking them to a secure safe house while the Met. moved against the Organization and the bent coopers who enable its top men to avoid successful prosecution. He was also intending to take a trip with Janina for a couple of days that would take them out of Plymouth.

The interview did not take long. Fortunately, the journalist was herself an experienced sailor, so he did not have to go into much detail and she was soon making her way back towards the quay. John had insisted that Janina wear a hair-concealing head-scarf and that they both wear sunglasses for the picture. He felt that few people in Plymouth will be looking at the 'Plymouth Live' web-site, and probably no-one at all beyond the City will access it.

They spent the rest of the day using the showers at the Marina and enjoying a stroll round the harbour area, finishing the day satisfying Janina's new found love of fish and chips.

John was up early the next day and when Janina woke she found a note telling her to get ready for a day at the seaside....

'So a surprise outing' she thought happily. But she had been concerned about continuing to carry the diamonds and Rahman's notebook around in her handbag. After looking over the boat she lifted a fender from the starboard side of the hull. Using the sharp sailor's penknife that she had found in the cabin she carefully opened the seam just sufficiently to slide in the notebook and the bag of diamonds. Although all she could find was sellotape to seal the slit she re-hung the fender over the side of the boat so that the slit was against the side of the hull, so unseen.

John returned to the Marina just as Janina was drying her hair following a shower.

'Right, if you are ready your carriage awaits madam' he said, when making a sweeping action with his arm, ending with his hand pointing as a small blue hired saloon parked on the quayside.

They crossed the wide River Tamar using the road-bridge alongside of which runs the Plymouth to Penzance railway. Ten miles further on, they turned off the A390 at the typically Cornish village of East Taphouse.

They then drove south following a series of ever narrower country lanes, across a landscape of undulating hills and mostly neatly farmed fields of various crops. All overarched by a clear blue sky.

Within about half an hour they came to the village of Polruan and found a parking place in the quaintly unkempt car-park on the cliff top from where they could look out over Lantic Bay in front of them and to their right the entrance to the River Fowey and Fowey Harbour, and beyond to the red and white tower marking Gribben Head.

Janina was quite taken with Polruan – if the length of lane running from the first house of the village down to the small, neat, harbour, must have been the steepest lane she had even seen.

After making their way down the lane they sat overlooking the range of water-based activities going on in the estuary. On a modest beach protected by the stubby, harbour wall, a group of youngsters were relaxing with ice creams, their brightly coloured kayaks pulled up onto the beach. Further out in the river numerous craft were bobbing at their swing moorings, with an occasional boat making a passage into or out of Fowey Harbour.

'Right' said John 'Now it's the ferry across to the town and your next surprise.' The ferry transported foot-passengers across the quarter mile of river separating Polruan and Fowey Town.

The ferry itself was a 30ft white-hulled clinker-built boat, skippered by a gray-haired ferryman whose nut-brown and heavily creased face suggested a long working life on the water.

Halfway through the crossing they could gain a sense of the wideness of the estuary. Looking down-river to the sea and up-river to the town itself and the river bending out of sight about a mile up river, just beyond the much larger vehicle ferry crossing from Fowey to a village called Bodinnick.

John knew that the large attractive house by the slipway where the vehicle ferry docked was appropriately called 'Ferryside'. And that it was the family home of the du Mauriers. A place where the novelist Daphne du Maurier lived for much of her life. Indeed, the imprint of Fowey and the surrounding villages, and indeed some other parts of

Cornwall, can be seen as a key feature of many of du Maurier's novels.

The foot ferry carrying John and Janina motored slowly toward the slipway with the skipper reversing the engine as he brought the boat gently to a halt. After disembarking, they climbed the short but steep slope leading from the river up to the narrow road that ran into the town centre.

'Come on' said John 'I want you to see the main quay, and we have some shopping to do.'

Even with the season coming towards an end the central square was still quite busy, with a mix of the more obvious tourists and less obvious townies. Out on the wide river a mix of scudding sailing dinghies, and larger more graceful sailing yachts, were enjoying a reasonable breeze – tacking into the wind with sails pulled in then turning, letting the boom swing out to spread the mainsail and so allow the boat to run downwind at speed.

After watching the boating scene for about ten minutes, John guided Janina into a nautical clothing shop.

'Not more tee shirts with printed messages reflecting a boating theme' sighed Janina.

'No look over there....that is what we require for this afternoon.' Laughed John, as he pointed at racks of female swim suits and male swimming trunks.

They left equipped with his and her Speedo swimming gear, two large towels, and a neat canvas knapsack to carry these.

John seemed to be getting quite excited as he led Janina back along the town road toward the ferry landing, but then he walked on past this for about ten minutes until they arrived at a picture-book little bay – with a fine-sanded beach, lapped by modest blue-green waves. To the right were a series of glistening rock-pools amongst a rocky section in the shadow of low cliffs – Tamarind bushes and the still heavily scented Cordyline palms were in abundance on the grassy verges lining the narrow lane by the beach.

'How very lovely! exclaimed Janina what is this place called.

'Well, it has the quite unusual name of 'Readymoney Cove', why such a name I do not know, perhaps it was landing stage for smugglers, so offering easy, 'ready', money for them.'

Within but a few minutes they had stripped off, preserving their modesty under their towels, and were in their swimming gear running down the beach and into the water. Just 30ft out from the beach they were able to swim.

John felt such a sense of relief as he enjoyed the physicality of the regular arm-crawling motion through the water. A relief gained as much of the tension that had built up over the past week eased. He first swam out to a cable, carrying a series of small white floats, running across the entrance to the bay. Placed there to ease the strength of incoming waves and so allowing water within the cove to be much calmer than it would have been if the waves had been free to drive in at full force.

After swimming strongly back and forth across the bay for the equivalent of about ten lengths of an average sized pool he turned over onto his back and just floated as he looked up at a blue sky clear of all but the occasional puff of white cloud and a few gulls wheeling in the thermals high above.

He noticed that Janina had swum out to a wooden diving platform anchored in the middle of the bay and was stretched out sunning herself.

He reflected on what a difference this last week had made for him..... his involvement with Janina had in effect taken his life and shaken it up big-time.

He knew that there was more to do before the adventure was concluded, but he also knew that he could never return to a life of working for his brother's business.

Having been rejuvenated by their swim, the pair were now enjoying ice- cream cones bought from the small cafe adjacent to the beach.

'What next?' asked Janina 'Back on the ferry to Polruan?'

'No' said John, 'I want us to relax after what we have been through and to have built up emotional resources sufficient to best prepare us for any challenges what might be still to come.

'I have booked us an estuary view room for the night in the Fowey Harbour Hotel, just back along the main street..... We will be sharing a room as I don't want you out of my sight for long.... but we do have twin beds. I was thinking that after spending a week together on a couple of smallish boats this would OK.'

'Of course John – Although I do feel much stronger now than when we first met, I still feel more secure if I can reach out and touch you......Just one thing John, whenever I mention problems you change these to challenges, is this an English language thing?'

'No' replied John with a twinkle in his eye. 'For a Marine any supposed problem is merely a 'challenge' to be overcome....You can leave the Marines, but the training and the mindset never leaves you!'

Feeling refreshed following their swim and rest they made their way to the hotel and after checking in were shown up to a spacious second-floor room with a panoramic view over the estuary mouth and across to Polruan.

By seven o'clock they were showered, had tidied up their somewhat creased clothes, and made their way down to the dining area with its well set out tables: with linen tablecloths, silver cutlery, and sparkling glasses. They settled down at a table by the window from where they could see some evening sailing activities, including a fleet of eight small dinghies that were obviously engaged in a race along the river.

'Those are Firefly dinghies,' said John; they used to be an Olympic class when raced single-handed but are now usually raced with a helm and a crew. They offer some lively sailing – I would think that those sailors are thoroughly enjoying their race.'

'I have never sailed before last week John, but I can see how exciting it can be, but also perhaps also dangerous..... But what does sailing mean to you?'

'I have been sailing since I was a young child, so there was no specific decision to take up sailing – I grew into it, first as crew for my dad then as a helm myself – it just seemed to be a normal aspect of growing up. When I am sailing into a decent breeze with the boat heeling off-wind – the tension of the tiller, the wind in your hair, and the occasional salty spray in your face.... there is just nothing like it. I know it sounds corny, but you do feel at one with nature during such times. In addition, the skills of navigation, sail setting, and of helming a boat, if done properly, do give a certain level of satisfaction.'

Janina could see from his eyes the joy he gained from a life-long love of sailing. She followed his glance down to the racing Fireflys, and just knew that he would have loved to be taking the helm of one of them – probably the one out ahead.

Suitably fortified with a substantial dinner, along with a bottle of decent red wine, they took a day's-end walk back down to Readymoney Cove along the heavily-scented lane over which bats flitted – they could also hear an Owl hoot-hooting in distance woodland.

The next morning they took their time to get showered and dressed, with each of them being drawn to gaze out of the window at the activities taking place on the river and on the stretch of water where the river merges into the estuary, it being today shrouded in a sea mist.

'The mist will burn off as the day warms up' said John. 'And the weather for the day is looking good.'

They breakfasted on fruit juice, poached eggs on wholemeal toast, and coffee and by 11 o'clock they had walked to the mouth of the river and so were looking out to sea. This morning a deep blue sea, its waves fringed with very light white foam. In order to get there they had followed a footpath that wound its way through a short stand of native British woodland lining the modest hill that rose up from Readymoney Cove.

At the top of the hill stood the fortified structure of St Catherine's Castle, another fortification paired with a similar fort, they could just about make out through the sea-mist, on the other side of the estuary. Both forts being built to prevent enemy ships from entering the harbour to attack Fowey-based ships at anchor or land-based military facilities.

John put his hands on Janina's shoulder and turned her to take in the view inland –

'Wow!' she said 'Quite a view' – They were looking up river, so over the Town of Fowey with its prominent church tower and jumble of riverside buildings, towards where the now broad river flowed from it source in the numerous tributaries first formed on Bodmin Moor.

'Well Janina, I hope you are up for a decent walk today....we are going back to Polruan, but we will be talking a circular route to get there'

'Sounds good to me after that dinner last night and today's breakfast I could do with some exercise.'

The walk began by their retracing the footpath down to Readymoney Cove then following the lane into the town. Where they bought some crusty rolls, a wedge of Cornish cheese, a couple of bananas, two bottles of apple juice....and a packet containing four 'saffron buns'. Something John explained as being a type of baked bun traditionally made and eaten in this part of the county.

They crossed the river on the solid vehicle ferry that connected Fowey with the village of Bedinnick about four times an hour during the hours of daylight. It was basically a floating platform design for function rather than elegance. Being secured during the crossing by two large chains that ran from shore to shore, lying on the riverbed. So all the captain had to do was start and stop the boat, the actual passage being guided by the chains. Along with the captain operating the boat from an elevated cabin on the starboard side were two younger crew members. One walking between the vehicles and foot passengers to collect the crossing fees, and in the process chatting cheerfully to both regulars and tourists.The other in charge of the gates at each end of the boat that required opening and closing for loading and unloading the cars, vans, and small lorries, that were packed neatly nose to tail along the three lanes of the platform for each trip. But this still left some space for motorbikes, cyclists, and pedestrians making the crossing.

As the ferry approached Bodinnick a large metal ramp was lowered and it scraped up the concrete slipway as the captain reversed the engines to bring the boat to a halt. The pair then made their way up the short stretch of steep slope past the 'Ferry Inn' and came to a path marked 'The Hall Footpath'

'I have made this walk a number of times.' said John

'Seeing the village again reminds me of a story told to me by the landlord of the Ferry Inn. It seems that this village saw an attempt in 1644 to kill the then King. A cannon ball was fired from the riverbank at the boat he was using to travel down river. It seems that the shot missed the King but managed to kill an unfortunate sailor.....if a true story it's a shame it was that way round. I would admit that I don't have time for the monarchy as an institution – it just emphasizes inequality'

'But surely John if you served it the British Army, didn't you fight for 'King or Queen and country?'

'Yes but when young you don't think too deeply about such matters and to be realistic in a Marine, or probably any military, unit you fight for the men alongside you. This has probably been the case from the earliest time of warfare..... the Athenian Phalanx, the Spartan Units, Roman Legions, and the Zulu Impi, being just some examples.'

The path they were following led up a gentle slope passing through some woods. After about half a mile the path flattened out and they were mostly above the tree covered hillside that they could see ran down to the riverbank below.

They came to a lookout position, one made obvious by a substantial seat set where it would take in the view down river, with Polruan on one side and Fowey on the other.

'Goodness John...... I am running out of English words to express just how beautiful this place is. The sun-sparkling river, the many colourful boats, and the surrounding scenery – the Lithuanian word would be 'lielisks'.'

It was this view from slightly changing angles they were able to look out on at times from the path which, in about three miles, sloped down again to arrive at an inlet leading from the main river. An inlet, 'Pont Creek', that must in the past have carried goods. Across a substantial foot-bridge was an old gray-stone building, clearly once a warehouse now converted into living accommodation. Having crossed over the bridge they sat on a grassy area to eat their late lunch. As they settled a large gimlet-eyed heron rose gracefully from the shallows and flapped its leisurely way down the creek.

After finishing their crusty bread and cheese, washed down with apple juice, John offered Janina one of the Saffron buns.

'This is a very local speciality...what do you think?'

She gently prised the bun open and after noting her surprise at its centre being made of a bright yellow dough, she broke off and tasted a small piece.

'It is different to anything I have ever tasted, but really fruity and it's nice to eat locally....yes its good. We do have many different types of pastries and buns in parts of Lithuanian, but nothing like these Saffron buns - even the name suggests something pleasant.'

'So what's next for us John?'

'Hm, it should be relatively straight-forward now. When we get back to Plymouth I will phone Nobby and try to find out when his specialist Serious Crime Squad unit can come to get us. Once in their protection I am that thinking that it will be a safe house for us until the most senior officers at the Met. have gone through Rahman's notebook and arrested the entire group of bent coppers and corrupt politicians noted in it. And have moved on to arrest Rahman and his gang for a range of criminal activities. We now have proof of diamond and people smuggling, money laundering, running illegal brothels and living off immoral earnings and criminal gains more generally, and also the protection racket.

I never myself dealt directly with a criminal organization as big as this one but I understand that when you start to take one of these apart people do come forward – even if to begin with this is only on a confidential basis. So the officers running the operation would then be able to collate various types of evidence, including no doubt bent police officers trying to reduce their own penalties, linking specific crimes to Rahman and his gang.

Hopefully, there will be sufficient evidence for a successful prosecution and very long prison sentences, as well as the progressive dismantling of the nation-wide drugs-trading. Perhaps other, more local gangs will move in but in the process of taking the Organization apart I would expect that they will identify how what must be a massive amount of drugs gets into the country each month. Taking out this supply-chain could make a significant mid to long-term difference to the street-level trade and its associated misery. Once Rahman is in custody we can look at getting you back to Lithuania.'

As John and Janina were relaxing in the mid afternoon at Pont Creek 250 miles away in the Argyle Square office, Ashif was glaring across his desk at the heavy weight core of the Organization. A group made up by Goldie, Zerya, Irvin, Joe, Kurt, Frank, Lewis, and Florin.

'So far then no fucking effective action to locate this slippery pair.' The gang members shifted uneasily in their seats, each finding interest in the wallpaper or the sky outside the window.

Zerya spoke up, as she gestured towards Joe and Irvin. 'If these two pricks had not assumed that they could take the pair in the pub on that crappy island we might have had a result.....mind you boss, we are somewhat hampered by not been allowed to go in with guns blazing, at least in public, which we can do in many other countries.'

'I accept the first point – that's the second time the pair have been underestimated and it must not happen again. As for the second point... it is what it is. They call it civilization. But you will be able to be very uncivilized once we have this pair in our hands.

Fortunately for you lot I have a contact that should be able to guide us to our prey.' He flicked on his intercom. 'OK Bill, I have finished bollocking these dicks, come in now'

Bill Gravney entered the office and Goldie got up to let him sit close to the desk on which the map used previously was spread out. 'Bill will be providing a link between the pair and ourselves, but first Goldie can you sum up where we are before we get to Bill'

It did not take Goldie long to admit that since losing them in Cowes they have not been able to find them again.

'This seems to suggest that they might have been at sea for some time. The problem for us will be if they decided to cross the channel or sail much further away. But, as they had to leave Lowestoft in something of a hurry they would presumably not have much in the way of provisions, or fuel, for their boat. This points to them landing at one of the south-coast ports such as – Exmouth, Torbay, Plymouth, Falmouth, Penzance – and we have operatives in each of these who have already been alerted to monitor all boats coming into the port.

The problem with the bigger ports such as Plymouth and Falmouth is that they have numerous places for a boat to dock. In addition, Plymouth is one of the places where Kurt has been overseeing action to take on a gang of would-be gangsters, so resources have been stretched.'

'OK' said Ashif 'So a possibility that we might spot them but even if we do we would still have a problem with taking them on in the public setting of one of these Marina things. I suppose we could just blow their fucking boat up but, although we can accept the loss of the diamonds and cash, we can't be sure that the notebook has been destroyed. I guess the reason they haven't sent the notebook to a senior Met. officer is that they can't be sure that any such parcel will not be opened by someone on our payroll, so we will assume they still have it..... which brings me to Bill.'

Bill explained how John had contacted him at New Scotland Yard six days previously and explained that he was on the run.

'He said that he and a woman were holding some valuable goods and a notebook that listed all of the Met officers and politicians currently being paid by the Organization – so fucking hot stuff – and as yet he has not identified me, presumably because he knows me as Nobby not Bill and that Ashif's handwriting is pretty bad.'

'John trusts me as an honest cooper' smirked Bill 'He remembered me when I was a naive poorly paid police officer not as now a wised up, flawed, but well rewarded and very happy human being.

As for their location – there has been quite a storm off the south coast and in his last call to me he said that if the weather conditions did get too bad they would seek shelter in the nearest port. So it could have been one of about half a dozen coastal towns in Dorset or Devon. But their original plan was to sail to Plymouth. So it does look like at some point they will turn up there....I am expecting John to call me quite soon now, but I think we should prepare for a trip to the seaside'

'OK' said Ashif 'We are now beginning to focus. I want you Louis and Florin to travel down to the Plymouth area and indentify a fairly isolated property on... what's it called the moor with the old prison in the center'

'Dartmoor' said Bill

'OK then Dartmoor..... Ideally it will be a holiday house that can be booked for a few weeks, but failing this just find any property and we will take care of the owners when we need to move in.'

'What about firepower?' asked Lewis.

'I do not feel like trusting you two pricks with guns, you Florin have already given one to the opposition. But as we don't know how this might pan out I want to be fully prepared.......Goldie has drawn up a list of armaments ......over to you Goldie'

Goldie stepped forward and read from a list called up on his phone.

'There will be a 9mm Koch pistol for each of us, with one in and one spare magazine each.

Four AK47s with 4 spare magazines each. We still have the two grenades taken to the Isle of Wight, and we are going to add four more to this, plus four smoke bombs'

You Lewis and Florin will not be armed until we join you, just in case you are stopped whilst looking for a house. We will be taking the two Range Rovers but all the arms will be shared out between two non-descript hatchbacks. One driven by Joe the other by Irvin. We will also maintain two-way radio contact once we are down there and encrypted phones until then.

Once we have definitely identified the location of the targets we will move, and move quickly.... Joe and Irvin to pick up the guns and bits from Park Royal and Zerya, Frank, and Kurt will take one Range Rover, with Bill and myself taking the other. I want you to return to your roots and think of this as a military operation – well prepared, efficiently and ruthlessly progressed, and successfully executed.'

'Right, mention of execution is where I think I should come in.' said Ashif. 'I will be joining this operation by helicopter once we have the targets in our control.....Goldie and I have been thinking about how we can carry out this action. Before I get to this I want to emphasise that the information that these two hold can cripple the Organization....the cash-cow whose rich production of money is made possible by us being one step ahead of the law and this is enabled by all of the coppers, like Bill here, that we have 'bent' towards our organization – so if you want to continue making money as you have been then we need to finish this now!'

Ashif dramatically brought his large fist down hard on the desk to emphasize the point.

'Let's assume that we have identified the boat - We then have two more obvious ways of organising the action. Firstly, as mentioned just now, we could just take dynamite and blow the boat to bits with them on it. Nicely simple and we will all be back in our London beds by the next day. But the problem with this is that we cannot be sure that the notebook is on the boat.... they might have posted it to a friend's or to Hardy's home, or even perhaps Janina's parents address in Lithuania....we just can't be sure it won't turn up again.

I am tempted to go for this option but, on balance, I prefer a second option. This being that we lift one of them – ideally Janina - from the boat and, if she has not got my property on her person you will pretty much take the boat to bits in searching for it. If you do find the goods then just eliminate Hardy and send him sailing off to meet his fucking maker. But, if you don't find the goods then we will assume that either Hardy has them or knows where they are. We will have the girl at the house and will then contact Hardy and threaten to torture then kill the girl if he does not hand over the book....I am pretty confident that this dick will want to come to her aid and so hand the goods over......perhaps foolishly assuming that his old ex-mate Bill here, or 'Nobby' as Hardy knows him, would not want be involved in a double murder........Once we have the book and diamonds Hardy will be eliminated......I will then fly down – so make sure there is adequate space for a helicopter landing in a quiet area on the moor, to be collected by one of you and driven to the house – Then we can all watch while Goldie, and any of you who fancy a turn, rape the girl, who I shall then strangle very very slowly. Her body will be loaded onto the helicopter, along with Hardy's, and both will be dumped at sea when we divert to fly over the coast before heading back to London. Then back to a focus on business as usual....any questions?'

'Seems pretty straight-forward to me said Zerya....providing that none of these pricks think they can take this guy on without sufficient back-up.'

'Too true' said Goldie. 'There might only be one of him but from now on we will treat this guy as serious opposition.'

The meeting broke up with Lewis and Florin preparing to leave for Dartmoor and Joe and Irvin to collect the two hatchbacks and then to the Park Royal unit where Benny should have filled the armaments order that he had already been provided with.

Back in Cornwall John and Janina had finished their late lunch and were continuing the walk along The Hall footpath, appreciating both the immediate scenery and the distant views across the estuary as they did so. Within another mile or so they were standing looking out over Polruan itself.

'Such a pretty little village' said Janina.

'Yes, pretty, but as you can tell by that large fishing trawler pulled up on the slip-way down there, this is still a work-place. Tourist and related activities might be the primary business of Polruan and indeed Fowey, but traditional marine-type work continues to have a place. Here it is repairing and maintaining fishing boats at C.Toms and Sons., whilst over in Fowey the focus is more of the same but with various types of sailing boats – and I know of two businesses in Fowey that still design and build traditional wooden rowing gigs and small sailing craft.

They walked back to the cliff-top car-park, seeing the sun sinking in the west as the long-shadowed evening was drawing in.

The next morning, now back at 'Sunrise', they woke to yet another sunny day and after John returned from a trip to buy milk, a loaf of French bread, and some croissants, they settled down for breakfast in the cockpit whilst observing the busy Marina with the occasional sailing boat leaving on the tide. Out in the main river a grey painted naval Destroyer class ship was making its sedate way out to sea.

'If OK with you John, I was going to get my hair done at that salon on the quay.'

'Seems fine to me, I shall have a wander around this side of Plymouth, it has been a while since I was last here, are you OK for money.'

'For sure, I counted Ashif's parting gift last night and we have £14,670 left in cash.'

'I was forgetting that....and talking about money reminds me that I need to pay our mooring fees, so I will call into the Marina office on my walk....I should be phoning Nobby to arrange the next stage of action against the Organization – including handing over the notebook and diamonds...I think you should keep the cash Janina to support you when you get back to Lithuania.'

Janina was looking thoughtful and John picked up on this asking.

'Are you having second thoughts about going home Janina?'

'I am not sure.....I do want to see my mum and dad but other than this there is little for me there, I am thinking that I might stay if I can get a work visa.'

'That should be possible, and I do have a spare bedroom in my flat so staying could be an option.'

'When will you be calling this Nobby then John?'

'I should do this within the next couple of days – I am pretty sure that, given the reach of their operation, Rahman and his cronies will soon locate us. But I am reluctant to set the next stage in motion as it will mean us having to stay in a safe house, and that could mean months of lockdown - Basically our being imprisoned until they have arrested and successfully prosecuted the top members of this criminal organization. It is so nice relaxing here......but we do need to trigger some action very soon.'

Janina went off to get her hair done and, after an hour or so relaxing and then tidying up the boat John went for a stroll along the quay, to the Marina office.

When John gave the name of the boat for which he assumed fees were due the staff member at the reception said that there was a note in her day-book so say that no fees were to be charged for 'Sunrise'.

'Any sailor prepared to put themselves in harm's way to save life is highly respected within the Plymouth sailing community. I think you can probably moor here fee free for as long as you want.'

After thanking the receptionist he left the office and set off along the path out of the Marina turning right towards the Hoe.

This walk was calling up memories from his time based here in 42 Commando. Although the camp was in Bickleigh, a few miles out of the city, they used to come to the Hoe at times for parades and to access the Marine's military vehicle store on the eastern side of the Hoe. He would also come to the Stonehouse facility for classroom based training and the occasional ceremonial duty. He could remember how the units would engage in some light hearted, if still competitive, racing up and down the 100 odd steps rising from the sea-level to the top of the Hoe.

On the way back to the boat he stopped to buy a take-away coffee from a cafe on the lower Hoe road. Then he walked to settle on a seat overlooking the Tamar Estuary. The seat was already occupied at one end by what John thought was a slim attractive lady who seemed to be lost in thought as she gazed out to sea. But as he sat down she briefly smiled up at him.

As he sipped his coffee he could sense the women staring at him rather intensely. He glanced at her and she immediately looked away and then back at him.

'Are you the sailor recently involved in a rescue in the Channel, I recognise you from a picture of you and your wife or partner on the 'Plymouth Live' web-site. Although I wasn't sure, as I think you were wearing sunglass in the picture.'

John looked directly into Jean's open face with its grey-flecked green eyes and he felt an immediate attraction.

'Yes, we did get caught up in a minor drama at sea a few days ago, but the women is neither my wife nor a partner, just a very good friend'

'Well, even allowing for some journalistic license, it seemed to have been considerably more than a 'minor drama'. So you are obviously staying in Plymouth just now.'

'Yes, for a few days probably...what about you, do you live here?'

'I work here but I have small cottage on the western edge of Dartmoor.'

John felt that he wanted to know more about this woman – He knew it was not his style, usually he would at best just exchange pleasantries with a stranger and move on.....but this felt different, he wanted to prolong the meeting.'

'So what type of work do you do?'

'I am a police officer based in an office over there.' she said pointing to the substantial stone–built ex-police station by the riverside.'

'What about you, what line of work are you in?'

'I have been working for my brother in an office-based job, but my experience over the past week or so had made me decide that I won't be going back to this....it lacks much in the way of stimulation. I will have to manage on my combined military and police pensions, such as they are, at least until I can find something.'

Jean immediately picked up on the police connection. 'So what policing were you involved with?'

John told her something about his work in the Met's Serious Crime Squad.

'So why did you take early retirement – you don't look all that old.'

'Well thank you for that' he smiled. 'I hate to say this but the Met. has too many corrupt officers......most are honest and committed to the job but some key positions do seem to be occupied by dubious individuals'

Why was he telling her all this stuff he thought.

'That's not a problem confined to the Met. we have similar issues down here.... the big fish in the drugs trade always seem to be one-step ahead of us and we just get to catch the occasional minnow' She was looking at her watch.

'Look I am sorry but I need to get back to the office as I have a phone call arranged with our ACC, but it has been lovely to meet you.'

'You too...perhaps I will see you again tomorrow'

As he watched Jean walk away he had a strange feeling in his stomach...

'What the hell's happening to me!'

Chapter Seven

The same day that John met Jean, the four friends had gathered together in Charlie's bed-sit eating take-away pizza washed down with cans of lager as they considered their situation.

'Look, I am sure something in going on around town......I have known Billy McDonnell since we were in care together and he gets his dough by selling mostly weed, but also some cocaine on the street. I think he wants to get out of this trade and he is working on his own addiction so that he can do without the money. Funny, that a bloke who had such a crap upbringing in care since the age of two, with no reason to respect anyone or anything, could feel guilty about trading drugs. Still the thing is that, apart from being told to look out for any local gangsters who seem to have come into money i.e. us.... Billy said that they have now also been told to look out for a sailing boat called 'Sunrise' with a couple in it that the Organization is seriously after. It seems that his controller, that prick Carl Kimble, has been bragging about his meeting the bosses of the Organization quite soon – it looks like Plymouth might be being honoured by a visit from criminal Royalty.'

'That's interesting Simmo' said Charlie.

'This might be our chance to really fuck the Organization – take out the bosses and perhaps also Carl Kimble and the other bastard that shot me....I am still getting scary flashbacks to that night.'

'Steady Charlie,' said Harry. 'Let's not get carried away – just think of the firepower they must have access too, all we have is a couple of old sawn-off shot-guns and we are not even that practiced at using these.'

'Look' interrupted Ross. 'I think that Harry's right, we would have trouble taking on a prepared force from this group but, given that we now have useful contacts with the local police, I think we can perhaps enhance the work of Jean's unit. Let's start by repeating our original tracing of their contact lines – if we are to get a visit from the top criminals there must be a reason for this and perhaps we can learn more about this than can the local coppers......Let's start by drawing up a rota to shadow Kimble – with you Charlie trying to restrain yourself from stuffing one of our shot-guns up his arse.'

So, beginning that evening, Simmo took the first eight hour shift in trailing the local controller...... and it was two days later on Harry's shift that Kimble met Florin and Lewis in a Union Street pub.

Harry called Ross and they agreed to wait and see what these three were up too before they alerted Jean, they also arranged for Charlie to join Harry with his motorbike so that they could follow the mobsters when they left the pub.

It was 11 o'clock before the trio came out of the pub, crossing Union Street to a parked van. The three of them getting into the front seats with Florin driving.

The van set off towards the northern suburbs on the Tavistock Road. But just two miles on they pulled into the car-park of a Premier Inn.

Harry and Charlie decided to assume that the three would be spending the night here so, after a call just to check in with Ross and Simmo, they headed back to Charlie's bedsit intending to get up early and be back watching the hotel by 6 am the following day.

It was a bleary-eyed pair that managed to be drinking coffee in a Costas just across the road from the hotel the next morning and from where they could just about see the white van. But it was four coffees each on, and some strange looks from the staff when, at 9 o'clock, they saw the three villains emerge from the hotel, get back in the van and re-join the Tavistock Road.

'That's a surprise' said Harry.

'I assumed they would be going back into town but instead they are heading towards the moor. Best keep quite a bit of space between us, we don't want to spook them.'

'I don't think these bastards would be spooked by two young blokes on an old motor-bike, but I get what you mean about not giving ourselves away.'

For the next three hours they followed the van on a route across the western side of the moor, at times doubling back on itself as if lacking any sense of where it was going. Charlie and Harry struggled to keep them in sight whilst also maintaining a sufficient distance to not alert the villains. At times they had to drive off the road and hide behind bushes as the van turned round to head back passed them.

'Bloody hell' said Charlie.

'They don't seem to know where they are supposed to be going, and we are going to need petrol very soon'

'Yes', 'It's as if they are looking for something. We will keep behind them for as long as we can.....they are obviously up to something' said Harry.

By midday the van pulled into the car-park of a tourist information centre in the central moorland village of Princetown. From where they walked the short distance to the same small cafe where the four friends had previously met Jean and Colin.

'Looks like its lunch time' said Charlie. 'Let's give Ross and Simmo a call and get them to bring us some petrol for our afternoon shift, there are no garages around here.'

So by the time the villains had finished their lunch and were back on the road the pair were following them with a fresh tank of petrol and having eaten the sandwiches brought by Ross and Simmo using the old borrowed Astra.

'You would think we could afford a decent car between us said Charlie given the dough we have stashed away.'

'Yes, but bear in mind our keeping a low-profile plan......our having to borrow Ted's old car for thirty quid a day plus petrol suggests that we are just as skint as we have ever been.'

The afternoon saw many more miles being covered, if mostly just retracing much of the morning's route then, about mid-afternoon, the van pulled up just past a substantial detached house on the outskirts of the village of Yelverton.

That's the third time we have been past that house and I remember they slowed to walking pace the second time. It does seem that that particular house is of interest for this bunch – perhaps they are going to break in and rob it...but why?' said Harry.

From where the pair were keeping out of sight they could observe the van and they saw Lewis get out, walk down to the house, and who then clearly took some pictures on his phone. He then walked up the long garden path and rang the doorbell. After a delay the door was opened by an elderly lady with a chain only allowing the door to be opened just a few inches.

Charlie and Harry could see that Lewis and the old lady spoke for a few minutes then he walked away and got back in the van.

Once settled he said.

'That's got to be one for us, some daft old biddy who when I asked if a Joe Green lived there just said no only herself and her husband. What a silly old cow – now we know that that big house with extensive grounds would be easy for us to take over......we probably only need the house for four or five days and if we do get any nosey callers while we are there we can either just waste them or hold them....its nicely secluded here'

The following morning over breakfast, John told Janina that he had decided that they should no longer delay calling Nobby as, for sure, the Organization would be closing on them.

'I would think that Nobby with the Met SCS team would probably be collected together and would then drive down to Plymouth overnight and be with us some time tomorrow.'

They spent the morning relaxing and reading... For John it was a James Bond book he found in the cabin and for Janina it was a couple of magazines bought with the fresh bread at the Marina shop.

Around midday John told Janina that he was just going for a walk and would phone Nobby when he got back.

His walk saw him retrace some of the route taken the previous day and he was hoping that Jean would again be sitting on the seat they had shared. His hopes were fulfilled when Jean greeted him with a welcoming smile and indicated for him to join her.

'It's lovely to see you again... I was hoping you would be here'

'It's good to see you too,' said Jean.

'I have been wondering why you are in Plymouth with a friend...in particular you said that your experience over the past week had made you determined not to go back to working for your brother.....now I could understand that the rescue might have perhaps given a different perspective on life, but you are obviously a very experienced sailor so I was thinking that the ...experience this week... that you alluded to was something more than the sailing'

'When we spoke yesterday Jean you mentioned issues with corrupt officers and the drugs trade......well over the last week we have been drawn into an aspect of the London drugs trade involving a significant criminal organization. But before I go into details can you say what your professional role is please.'

Jean looked into John's face and this impression, and what he had said the previous day about police work, made her judge that he was someone to be trusted.

'Look, I should probably not be telling you this but I am an acting Chief Inspector and I have been put in charge of a newly formed unit tasked with significantly disrupting the drugs trade in the south-west region, a trade that has been doing progressively more damage to the lives of young people over the last few years......We have a small team of specially selected officers based in the office over there and if, as yet, we have not made much progress, we have started to identify local operatives. And we have contact with a local group that have already taken it in their own hands to disrupt the trade, with one of them just about surviving being shot......John, just now you mentioned a significant criminal organization...does that link to organization as in 'The Organization' with a capital O?'

'Yes...it is a group known as the Organization, headed by a nasty piece of work named Ashif Rahman, that we are running from. But we have now been in touch with a trusted officer in the Met who has spoken with his seniors, up to the Commissioner herself I understand, and we are expecting that a team of SCS officers will soon be coming to our aid.'

'Look John, can you come to a meeting tomorrow so that you can brief us on as much as you know about the Organization and we might be able to give you some intelligence we have gained from the young men I mentioned just now about the criminal organization's chain of control.

'I will need to talk with Janina about this but I don't see any problem with our meeting up.' Adding with a cheeky grin, 'Any excuse to see you again is useful...'

On their parting Jean made her way back to her office and John walked further along the coastal road around the Hoe in order to make the call to Nobby. He made the call whilst looking out to the calm, gray, sea with Drakes Island to the right.

'Nobby answered within two rings of the call. 'Hi Nobby, how are you getting on with the Met team?'

'Hi John, all good - green light from the very top and we have a safe house already prepared for you and the girl in Kent, with the SCS having a plan to move on Rahman and his merry men, including the corrupt officers, once we have the notebook and the diamonds. In the meantime, I have a crack team set up and we can be ready to move within a few hours - Just give me your location and we will be there ASAP.'

'Right.... we are moored in the Mayflower Marina on the western side of Plymouth – it is quite a busy Marina, so best to take a low-key approach. It's late afternoon now so probably best if you can get here by lunch time tomorrow.'

'Sounds good to me....see you very soon John.'

'After ending the call John reflected that lunch-time tomorrow at least allows me to see Jean before we go into secure lock-down.'

That evening John and Janina decided that in what would probably be their last night of freedom for some time they would enjoy a fish and chip supper in the floating restaurant moored further up the River Tamar. Just by an area of Stonehouse barracks that had been given over to residential and leisure development.

Settled at a solid wooded table suiting the rustic decor of the restaurant, they ordered their meal and were quietly reflective as they each thought about what the next couple of months will hold.

'Once we get to the safe-house we will make a plan of action,' said John

'I would think that when we were sure that Rahman and his cronies were in secure custody we could think about leaving the house. Possibly a trip back to Lithuania, and after you show me the sights I can leave you to stay with your mum and dad. You can fly back to Britain for the trial and to see that the criminals have been locked up for good. Then you can make a decision on whether you return to your country or stay on in Britain......for now let's enjoy our last night of freedom for a while...... tell me what you are thinking apart from our immediate situation'

Janina lent forward, 'I have been bursting to tell you about Ben......'

'Ben who?'

'I think you know Ben who, John – Ben of the Isle of Wight, Ben of the big brown eyes, Ben of the sexy smile.....that Ben.'

'Oh yes, that Ben' grinned John. 'So what about him?'

'Do you remember that during the hours we were moored by Hurst Point you gave me his e.mail address and phone number. Well after I had my hair done yesterday I was feeling pretty self-confident and I thought I would call him using the Marina pay-phone. And although at first he was surprised, he seemed to be quite pleased that I had called. He did ask how the runaway lovers i.e. us were doing but I soon clarified our relationship and explained that we just had to get away from the bad guys. I said that perhaps one day I would be able to tell him why we were being chased. We ended up chatting for about an hour and agreed to talk again very soon.'

'Well, I did think that you were taking a long time at the hairdressers, but as that sort of place is a mystery to me I assumed two hours to be normal......I am very pleased that you made contact, he seems to be a sound bloke and I remember how doe-eyed he was when he looked across the pub table at you, so I am not surprised about his being pleased to hear from you.'

After coffee and complimentary mints they made their way slowly back to 'Sunrise' and settled down for the night.

When they got up the next morning the steady drizzle suited their lowish mood.

'We should be pleased that the cavalry are coming over the hill to save us' said John.

'Yes,' agreed Janina 'But it does bring an end to what has been the most exciting time of my whole life.'

John left quite early, telling Janina that he was due to meet-up with Jean later on in order to exchange information about the Organization .... possibly to make her local action more effective and possibly for us to gain some useful information we can pass on to the Met. team.

But the meeting was not until 12 noon and he had a personal mission to complete before then. He assumed that following his chat with Nobby the Met team would not get to the Marina until the early afternoon. He left his mobile and suggested to Janina that she might like to call Ben from the boat during the morning.

'Sounds good to me, see you later John'

John's mission led him into town to seek out a jewellers shop and in the main shopping area of the city he found what he was looking for. A jewellers with a large clock attached to a sign hanging over the impressive wood and glass door.

The two broad front windows on each side of the door were full of various valuable goods - sliver table-ware, christening and anniversary presents, trays of rings, watches, bracelets, ear-rings, necklaces and broaches......all lit by subdued yellow lighting.

It did not take him long to complete the transaction and, after spending an hour or so reading the daily paper over coffee in a small cafe overlooking the restored Barbican area of the city, he casually walked to Jean's office for the 12 o'clock meeting.

In the office Jean was awaiting a call back from Peter the ACC in answer to a query she had e.mailed to him first thing that day. Her thoughts were interrupted by Colin leading Ross and Simmo into her office.

Jean had also asked Ross and Simmo to join the meeting so that all three perspectives related to taking on the Organization could contribute to the discussion.

John arrived soon after and once the coffee and tea had been sorted and Jean had made the introductions, she opened the meeting by briefly outlining the progress her Unit had made so far. Offering her apologies for lack of progress.

'But we have only been operating as a Unit for two weeks now and following the supply route beyond Carl Kimble is our next step.'

Ross started to explain about the word on the street being about some significant action involving the top villains in the Organization...... but they were interrupted by an officer coming into the room to say that the ACC was on the phone and would like a word with Jean immediately.

'Sorry Ross, but can you just wait a minute while I take this call.'

Within just two minutes Jean was back looking quite agitated.

'Look John, when you told me about a SCA unit coming down from London on a drugs-related matter I was curious to know why we had not heard about this. So I asked my ACC if he had simply omitted to alert us. It turns out that neither the ACC nor the Chief Constable knew anything about this cross-border police action. Well of course an alarm was ringing now and they contacted the Met. Commissioner and she was also in the dark'......as Jean was speaking John was already up, out of the door, and running towards the Marina.

When Jean, Ross, Simmo, and Colin caught up with him he was standing in the cockpit of 'Sunrise' looking at a scene of devastation.... almost all of the boat's fittings had been broken off and the internal furnishings had been ripped apart.

'What a fool am I' cried John.

Jean saw a letter taped to the tiller. 'Here John they seem to have left you a message.'

He tore the letter open and read a short message.

'Hi John old mate

As you now know, we have the girl and if you want her back in one unravaged piece you need to do exactly what I say. We have left your mobile phone and I will call you soon.

Nobby... but not the Nobby you once knew John'

John screwed-up the letter in his fist, his face set in determined anger.

Jean took his hand. 'Look John, they have Janina but at least they seem to be looking for a deal'

During the 3-4 hours that John had been in the City, and at the meeting, the two black Range Rovers had pulled into the Marina car-park.

Leaving Zerya, Frank, and Kurt by the cars, Goldie and Bill walked along the moorings until they came to 'Sunrise' to find Janina sitting in the cockpit.

Bill pulled out his warrant card and said to Janina that they had met John as they were driving though the City so he was already in their charge. 'As soon as we make contact in a witness protection programme we have to keep all potential witnesses out of sight.

So he is in one of the cars over there....if you can just bring the goods and some clothes for a few days you can join him.'

Something about the situation made Janina uneasy – the second man did not look much like what she thought of as a policeman so, although she decided to accompany them to the car, she would just check to see if John does want Ashif's property handed over.

When they got to the car-park she could not see into the car due to its smoked windows and as she resisted the gentle pressure from Bill trying to encourage her into the car, Zerya and Kurt just lifted her bodily and bundled her in. These two then got in each side of her, with Goldie and Bill climbing into the front seats.

Goldie grabbed Janina's handbag and shook the contents out onto the seat – 'Nothing here for us for fuck's sake..... rip her bloody clothes off and see if you can find anything.'

Goldie was furious but Bill was calmer 'Hang on, let's just take a few minutes to assess where we are..... we have the girl, but not the goods, They could still be on the boat so we can pull it apart. Failing this Hardy must have them so we can either risk a shoot–out – he still has the Koch pistol - when he comes back to the boat, or we can take her to our new house and hold her hostage until the dickhead delivers the goods.'

'Good thinking Bill' said Goldie – 'You two....take the bitch to our new holiday home and me, Frank, and Bill will go over the boat. If Hardy does turn up while we are there he can't do anything as we have the girl. And make sure she remains unharmed for the time being according to Ashif's orders.'

Within an hour the boat had been thoroughly but unsuccessfully searched, the letter left, and Bill, Frank, and Goldie were also on their way out of Plymouth heading towards Yelverton and Dartmoor.

Up on the moor earlier in the day Florin, Carl, and Lewis, had driven straight into the long drive of the house they had identified as their base. An old man was tending to some roses and he walked towards the van and asked them what the hell did they think they were doing.... Florin just punched him very hard in the face and dragged him into the house. Within minutes they had the elderly and very frightened couple locked it the copious cellar with a bottle of water, a loaf of dry bread, and a bucket to use as a toilet.

'You two will be staying here for the next few days so get fucking used to it.'

'Why don't we just shoot the couple now?' asked Lewis 'Well, if things go pear-shaped we might need them as hostages, or to answer the door if nosey neighbours come calling.'

'Yea...... I see what you mean...... they have seen our faces so we will have to shoot them before we leave......the nearest neighbour must be about a quarter of mile away...... it looks like this was once a smallholding.'

Following a phone call the two hatchbacks also drove into the house's driveway and Joe and Irvin unloaded the weaponry.

'Right' said Florin. 'You three get these cars back up on the moor in one of the isolated car-parks, take the van to bring you back. We don't want to draw unnecessary attention by turning the property into a car-park and the Range Rovers will be here quite soon.'

Back in the Marina Jean sat alongside John in the cockpit – he ran his hands through his hair and was clearly distressed.

'Look John...don't blame yourself, these people were determined to get to Janina, at least they have not shot you to get at her which they might well have done if you had stayed on board. You are still alive and between us we can work out a plan.'

'But we don't even know where they are holding her.'

'I would think that the Marina probably has security cameras monitoring vehicles coming and going so we should be able to identify the car or cars they were using, and then we can analyse recordings of traffic cameras located on the roads leading out of the City. So then be able to identify the direction they took ....it is at least a start.'

'That might not be necessary' interrupted Ross.

Who, with Colin, Simmo, and Jean had followed John when he ran to the boat.

'Jean turned to look at him but John kept his head down until he heard Ross say 'I think I know where they might have taken her.' Then his head shot up 'Where, where...?'

'Me, Simmo, and our other two friends that Jean and Colin know have been following a local drug dealer called Carl Kimble, a right shit. He works for the Organization and in order to help Jean and Colin's work we have been tailing him to see if we can identify the supply lines that would have changed after our previous action to disrupt the trade. Two days ago we followed him to a meeting with a couple of obviously hard bastards in a Union Street pub.

Following the get together they then drove to a Premier Inn hotel on the Tavistock Road. Now we were sure they were up to something, and bear in mind we had already been hearing about local underworld rumours suggesting that some big shots of the Organization were due to pay a visit to the City.

Early the next day, so yesterday, we staked out the hotel and when they left we followed them up onto the moor....they drove around for hours mostly in circles, stopping seemingly at random outside some larger houses. After about six hours of this they then parked outside a house that they had driven past twice earlier in the day. One of them then approached the front door of the house then got back in the car and they drove straight back to the Premier Inn. Where we assumed they would be spending the night.

We decided not to tail them the next day due to Charlie having to go back to hospital for physio, Harry having taken his mum shopping and me and Simmo having arranged to come here for our meeting. We decided to take a 24 hr break and start again tomorrow.'

'So' interrupted Colin 'You think this house might be serving as a base for the group. I guess they would want somewhere quite isolated but still near the City while they operated down here.'

'Could be' said Simmo.

'It seems that at the very least we should take a look' said Jean.

Just then John's phone rang and he answered immediately.

'Hi John mate' said Bill.

'You bastard' John replied – 'I trusted you to be a straight copper'

'Yea, sure, but being straight doesn't pay many bills John.... Let's say I stopped being a timeserving sucker....anyway cut the shit, we need the goods that you have and you need to deliver them to us within 24 hrs or we leave here leaving behind a very dead woman.'

'If you or anyone else harms a hair of her head I promise that I will hunt you down.'

'Right cut the tough-guy crap, when do we get the goods?'

Jean was standing in front of John mouthing 'more time'.

'Look, the goods are not here. We thought that Rahman's men might get to us so I sent them in a package to a friend in Torquay. I will need 72 hours to drive there and back and then make an arrangement to meet you. I am not just going to hand the goods over until I am sure that Janina is safe.'

'You have 48 hours and any tricks and she is dead – I will call in exactly two days and be ready to make the swap'

The phone cut off and John turned to Jean... 'Can we go and look at the house that these guys have located?'

Jean, Ross, Simmo, and John were soon on their way to the location just beyond Yelverton that Charlie had phoned through to them. They were using an unmarked BMW previously allocated to Jean's new drug squad. John was staring at the passing scenery but was also thinking about a possible strategy for freeing Janina. He was pretty sure that even if he could hand over the goods, they would still kill Janina and no doubt himself. But he did not even know where the bloody goods were.

'Surely' he thought. 'If she had them with her they would already have found them.'

'They drove past the house and stopped just out of sight, with John, Jean, and Ross, careful making their way to a space between the roadside hedge from where they could gain a better view. The two Range Rovers were a pretty obvious sign that this was where Janina had been taken.

Jean could sense John's tension.

'No John we can't make a move now, we need to think through how we proceed.'

'You are right Jean....We best go now as I am having trouble staying in control. These guys are going to be seriously armed.'

'Let's go to the cafe in Princeton to consider where we are.'

Once settled into the cafe, Jean led the assessment. She had already been updated by her office that CCT cameras at the Marina had identified the Range Rovers and six occupants.

'So, assuming that one of the six was Janina, we have the five from the Marina and the three scoping for the house in the van yesterday, so at least eight and I think that we should assume possibly up to ten. We only have about 44 hours now before the deadline. The normal procedure would be just to surround the house and try to negotiate but I think this bunch would probably try to shoot their way out potentially causing serious harm to police officers.........
And even if we were to rely on police resources, it would take time to organize this and realistically we would probably have to get the anti-terrorist squad down from London.'

'I think we need help from the military' said Colin.

John had seemed to be somewhat distant while they were talking then he looked at Jean.

'Yes, Colin is right....we need the Marines, they have a very local presence and I think I know who to make initial contact with.'

He quickly made a phone call, explaining to the others that he was phoning an old friend, Lt Colonel James 'Spike' Callaghan, leading officer of 42 Commando Battalion based in Bickleigh Barracks, not far from Yelverton.

Following the call, he told the others that he had arranged to see James first thing the following day – that's the earliest he can get back to the Bickleigh base from an exercise in Snowdonia. As you could hear, I have briefed him on the mission I want him to think about. He did say that he suspected there would be masses of bloody red-tape and related paperwork.'

'So in the meantime' said Jean. 'I will contact my senior officers as they do need to liaise with The Met and the Home Office, and the Ministry of Defence will need to be involved if British troops are to be deployed in active service on British territory.'

The evening was drawing in now as the police BMW made its way back to the City. Before the group broke up John thanked Ross and Simmo for finding the house. Ross asked if there were any way that the four friends could be involved in action at the house.... but were told by Jean that this would not be possible.

Given the mess that the boat was in, Jean asked John if he would like to spend the night at her cottage. 'I have a spare room and you are welcome to use it.'

'I think that I would like some company tonight please Jean, it's going to be a long night and I doubt that I will be able to get much if any sleep.'

Between them they did get some sleep, due more to a reaction to the stress of the day just gone, and over breakfast they focused on the day ahead.

'You take the MG John, and I will arrange for a patrol car to take me to the Crownhill Headquarters where I am due to meet with our Chief and Assistant Chief Constables to co-ordinate the official arrangements for deploying a Marine unit. Whilst you meet the battalion commander in order to plan operational details. We will be using some PCO19 officers in fast pursuit cars, just in case any of the villains do manage to break out and we need to chase them.'

As they prepared to leave John took hold of Jean's hands, thanks for all of your help Jean.'

'I suppose that it is really only part of my work, if in rather exceptional circumstances.'

They held eye contact for long enough for each of them to know that their relationship was going beyond just work.

John arrived at the entrance to Bickleigh Barracks just ten minutes before the prearranged 9 o'clock meeting. He could not help but notice the Marine motto in gold lettering over the heavy gates '*Per mar, Per terran*' By sea by land.

The Duty guard was expecting him and he was cleared within minutes and directed to the main office block. From the front office he was taken straight through to the Unit Commander's office.

'Hi Jonno really good to see you....looks like you are causing quite a bloody stir, I have already been ordered to cooperate fully with you, although we have not officially been given the go-head just yet.'

'Hi Spike, or should I address you as Colonel Callaghan....you are looking pretty good, if perhaps a bit fuller on the waist-line.'

'It's got to be 'Spike' for us two John, we go back a long way – and yes there is an inch to two on the waist since we were in service together as captains in Iraq and perhaps even three inches since we were finishing our basic Marine training together in the King's Squad at Lympstone.....Let's order some coffee and you can explain more about what you want from us. I have asked a couple of officers, Jim Dowd for logistics, Nic Hamilton who will be in overall command on the ground, and also Sergeant Clem 'Mac' Mackenzie' to join us. I think that Mac could well be leading any actual assault – he is a top Marine and bloody tough.

I would love to be directly involved in the action but, given my position, I am afraid I will have to oversee the op. from a distance and look on enviously whilst parked up about two miles away on the moor with you Jonno. Mind you it will be useful for the officers as well as the 'bootnecks' to get some live action'

'Wha.....' interrupted John 'There is no way I will not be in the assault team – Chief Inspector Jean Boyd is in the process of seeking approval for me to take part – she is presenting my case on the basis of my personal involvement and previous military and police service, both in armed roles. And I can play the Victoria Cross Award card. It's the first time that award might turn out to be useful.'

'Why does that not come as a surprise to me Jonno, I should of known that you would not be prepared to just be a spectator when a match is on!'

It was just before lunchtime when the Marines and John had finished pouring over a rough map of the immediate area around the house and of the wider terrain beyond, and to have formulated at least a working plan, with the intention to launch the assault at first light the next day. This time being chosen on the assumption that the baddies would be at their least alert at that time, and it was hoped that an early morning moorland mist might have formed.

The group broke up with Jim going off to sort out vehicles, body armour, weapons and ammo beyond the standard personal issue, and other necessary equipment, and with Nic and Mac going off to select and prepare a team of ten Marines.

'OK Jonno, we will be ready to move early tomorrow but we now have the rest of today to click our heels as we wait for the official order to go ahead with the op. Come and have a look round 42 Commando Brigade HQ, it will be a walk down memory lane for you. Let's grab some lunch in the Galley and then I will show you round.'

It was the case that John was soon reflecting on his time during the 32 weeks of basic training, considered to be toughest basic training of all the NATO forces, which probably means the toughest of any of the World's armies. In front of them, a new group of recruits were making something of a mess as they attempted to run the challenging assault course – 'Christ were we as bad as that when we first signed up Spike?' – 'Well each generation of Marines thinks that they were fitter and harder than the next lot' he laughed.

'Thanks Spike, the intensity of the planning earlier and the walk around the base has distracted me, at least somewhat, from concerns about Janina.'

'That's fine Jonno..... look I have just been paged about an incoming 'top security' call – this will be the news we have been waiting for.

Grab a coffee, and I will meet you in the main hall as soon as.'

After visiting the Galley John was looking at the long list of campaigns that marked the history of the Royal Marine Regiment; a record carved in a pair of highly varnished shield-shaped mahogany tablets set each side of the broad chimney breast at one end of the hall. Even in the new century he could see deployments to Iraq, Afghanistan, Kuwait, and very recently a peacekeeping deployment with the Byelorussian 103 Parachute Regiment under the auspicious of the UN.

Just then Spike strode into the hall.

'We have the go ahead Jonno, providing we can move any neighbours within a one mile radius and we must do our utmost to contain any fire-fight to the property itself.

The Devon and Cornwall Chief Constable and the Met Commissioner were both party to the Skype call and they seem to be raring to close down this Organization. They are confident that if they can get the stuff that you have, and arrests were made out of the hostage taking, then they can move quickly and effectively.....the Chief Constable will be ensuring that the near neighbours will be taken to a local hotel tonight. They did mention that the boss of the criminal organization seems to have disappeared – he is not at their base in London.........We now have about 12 hours and need to grab a few hours sleep before we finalise our preparations'

'I think that you should bed-down at my quarters tonight Jonno, the wife won't mind, she is used to last minute arrangements.'

'Good idea, thanks Spike, I want to call Jean and then have a quick briefing with Captains Jim and Nic and also Sergeant Mac.'

The briefing was needed just to finalise who did what during what would be a carefully choreographed assault –

It was 4 am when these four, along with their commander, were gathered again, this time being joined by 10 tough looking Marines. In addition, there were 2 Met and 2 Devon and Cornwall SC019 police officers.

John looked at the group, he was pleased but not surprised to note no nervous shuffling of feet here, no sign of pre-action nerves.... just a look of determined alertness on the face of each man.

After one more run through the operational plan they put on light weight body armour, strapped gas masks onto their belts, checked the action of their 9mm hand-guns and the semi-automatic rifles capable of single shots and short bursts of fire, and of course each of the Marines had a lethal dagger, the emblematic weapon of the Regiment. They also had two underslung grenade launchers and two dozen smoke canisters plus launchers.

Jim stepped forward.

'We have two personnel carriers...you four plus Mac in one and you four and John in the other. The two remaining Marines were each allocated to accompany the police officers in two four-by-fours.

Jean, Colin, and Peter the local ACC, would soon arrive at the base to join the unit Commander and to follow the operation via two-way radios and via Nic with a transmittable body camera.

Right we want to rescue the girl and also the elderly home owners if they are still alive. Do not hesitate to shoot anyone else on sight...to kill, not to wound. These are dangerous people.'

The vehicles were lined up in the yard and John, now with an automatic rifle to compliment the Koch pistol he had gained back in Lowestoft was dressed in full Marine battle fatigues, if stripped of regimental badges.

He was looking forward to the action and to taking on the very nasty people holding Janina he was especially determined to catch, or if necessary kill, Nobby.

The convoy moved off and stopped two miles from the house in the centre of the tiny village of Mevey with John, and the eight Marines led by Mac, setting off down the lane at a steady trot. About one mile from the house four plus John peeled off to approach the house from the rear and the other five Marines stopped at one hundred yard intervals to work their way through the hedge bordering the front of the property.

John and the four tasked with a rearward approach also fanned out and 10 minutes before their synchronised watches would indicate the time to begin the final approach, all of the men were in place. So, within twenty minutes of leaving the people carriers the house was surrounded and the would-be assault group had taken up prone positions about five hundred yards from the house.

John was feeling a tightness in his stomach muscles similar to what he remembered from his time in the regiment, in those quiet few minutes just before an operation.

There was, as they hoped, a light mist and two of the Marines crawled slowly forward to take up positions against the walls of the house ready to launch smoke canisters through the windows. And two plus John at the rear and two plus Mac at the front, began to crawl slowly forward. The ones left at the back and the front were placed to stop any of the enemy leaving the house once the action began.

What they didn't know was that Ross, Simmo, Charlie, and Harry, had yet again borrowed the old Vauxhall Astra and were now parked on a low moorland hill from which, with the aid of binoculars, they could observe the house. Ross knew about the 48 hour deadline and had worked out that either sometime during the night or early this morning there would be action taken at the house. They decided to take a chance that this would not kick-off until daylight as the glasses they had borrowed did not have night-vision so there would have been little point in their coming before now.

There was some argument in the car about whose go it was for the five minute turns with the glasses that they had agreed on. But, as each one was taking their turn they were expected to keep up a running commentary about what was going on, they were all sort-of being kept informed.

In the house's kitchen Bill and Goldie were having a smoke with their first coffee of the day when Goldie's phone rang. It was Ashif.

'It's me Goldie, we are about ten minutes away from you, Hardy's time runs out this afternoon so we can entertain ourselves with the bitch until he shows up with the goods – as we are going to kill them both he won't be seeing her. Get her stripped and ready, but don't do anything until I get there.'

'Check boss, see you soon.' As he put the phone down on the table Goldie smiled....looking forward to the next few hours, rape was a sexual normality for him.

Just then they heard Nic's voice from a loudspeaker.

'You people in the house, you are surrounded, and I am calling on you to all come out in single file with your hands up and leaving all of your weapons and any hostages in the house – come out now!'

'Fuck it' said Goldie 'As he ran to the bottom of the stairs shouting to the others to get armed. He felt confident that they could take on the police. We have sufficient armament to take on a bunch of fucking PCO19 pricks.'

As the gang were hurriedly taking up firing positions Bill grabbed Goldie's arm, he was now feeling right out of his depth – 'The games up Goldie, we should give up now and hand the girl and the old couple over unharmed.'

Goldie looked Bill directly in the eyes as he brought up his pistol and shot him, once it the chest and then in the head.

'I fucking hate coppers straight or bent, and I hate fucking cowards even more.'

Zerya was by an upstairs rear window and she spotted a slight movement of one of the Marines positioned about five hundred yards from the house. Her trained eye then picked out the other two Marines and John. 'Goldie' she shouted they have military support but only four at the rear.'

'At least two more here at the front' shouted Irvin. He was unable to see the two Marines flattened at each side of the house.

Goldie assumed that the police and military had underestimated their strength – just seven fucking marines and no doubt a few SCO19s – we can take them on and at least a couple of us might get clear.'

He went to the front door opening it just enough to get the barrel of his AK 47 clear.

'Go fuck yourself; if you try to get in we will shoot the old couple and the girl.'

This was the pre-planned trigger for Nic to blow a whistle as a signal for windows to be smashed and smoke canisters thrown in, immediately followed by a full-scale assault back and front to begin.'

The next five minutes saw all hell break loose – Bullets flew both towards and from the house – two Marines went down – But those remaining burst through the front and back doors, taking no prisoners, and shooting one villain after another as they rapidly worked their way through the building.

When two Marines kicked in the living room door they found Florin and Carl, having discarded their guns, were already kneeling on the floor with their hands raised.

John was calling for Janina but had no response as he took the stairs two at a time with Mac hard on his heals – Kicking open a bedroom door they were confronted with Goldie holding Janina in front of him as he pointed a pistol at her head.

'I want a Range Rover ready to go within five minutes or she is toast'.

John was unsure how to deal with this but Janina moved fast as she brought her elbow hard into Goldie's stomach, he barely flinched but it gave Mac just sufficient clear sight to fire a short burst of his automatic, with one bullet smashing though Goldie's shoulder. He staggered back, dropping his gun.... then knelt down on one knee, obviously in some pain.

Janina rushed to John and they clung together as tried to calm her down. Mac stood over the wounded Goldie who was cursing in pain. The Marine then fired two shots into his head.

'Not Geneva Convention arsehole, but justice can at times be rough – it's hell for you sonny, not prison.'

The mopping-up operation was efficiently carried out. The elderly couple were quite distressed but relieved that their imprisonment had been ended.

Florin and Carl were sitting hand-cuffed in the back of one of the police cars and of the others: Goldie, Lewis, and Irvin, were dead and Joe, Frank, and Zerya, were seriously injured. The Marines had taken three casualties – one critical, two less serious.

Hearing the sound of a helicopter John looked up as the copter circled over the scene twice and then flew east. Jean had arrived at the house and was helping Janina to an ambulance – but she turned at the sound of the copter.

'John, that's Rahman I was mocked by Goldie that when his boss flew in they would start assaulting me.'

John swore under his breath 'Looks like he has seen our action and is now getting away. I wonder where the copter comes from.'

'Perhaps it is the Biggin Hill airport that I used to hear them talking about, many trips were made from there.'

'Right said John we will head there.' A quick chat with Nic, and with Jean's cooperation, John with Mac as a passenger, was driving one marked police BMW across the moor followed by another being driven by Colin with a PCO19 officer beside him and three burly Marines squashed in the back seat.

Up on the moor the four friends had gotten quite excited watching the action rage below.

'What's going on down there?' said Harry pointing to the road below them. A figure was running along the road and through the binoculars they could see that he was carrying a AK47. As they were watching, he walked out in front of a car that was driving across the moor. When the car stopped, he opened the driver's door and hauled the driver onto the road. As the driver resisted, he was hit hard in the face with the butt of the gun. The figure then got into the car and set off with wheels spinning as it accelerated down the road. In the fog of battle, Kurt had managed to slip away from the back of the house and was now escaping.

'That's the bastard that shot me' said Charlie 'He is on the run.'

'Not if we can help it' said Simmo, as he slammed the Astra into gear and ran it down to the road.

It took five miles of hard driving for them to catch the fleeing car, with the Astra being pushed to its very limits. Simmo might have been a bit 'daft', as he had often been described, but he was a very good driver and on the twisty moorland roads he had the advantage. As he pulled alongside the fleeing car Kurt aimed his gun and fired a short burst. Most bullets went wide but one crashed through the window on one side and exited by the window on the other.

Charlie fired the shotgun and, although the resulting explosion and smoke nearly overwhelmed the four, Simmo was able to smash into the fleeing car, pushing it off the road for it to career down a slope and straight into a decent-sized tree.

The four spilled out of the Astra and running to the crashed car they pulled an unconscious Kurt from the wreck.

Charlie pointed the shotgun at his head but Ross grabbed the barrel saying.

'No Charlie, this guy is going to serve a very long prison sentence for what he had been involved in today and for shooting you. Let's not step over the line'

'OK' said Charlie as he kicked Kurt very hard in the stomach. Ross then called Jean to let her know that another gang-member had been caught.

Once they joined the A38 the two BMWs made good time with the road ahead being cleared by their 'blues and twos'. They took the M5 past Exeter before following the A303 towards the M3 and London. On the way Mac called the Marine base where Jean, with senior offices, both local and from London, had gathered. Mac turned his phone onto speaker so John could hear and they learned that Jean's ACC had called the Met. and that the Met was in the process of contacting Biggin Hill airport to tell them to refuse take off clearance for Rahman's private plane – but cautioning airport security not to challenge his party directly.

As the cars were speeding up the M3 John turned to Mac.

'No complaints Mac, but why did you waste that guy back at the house.'

Mac breathed deeply.....'As you know we are trained to remain calm in the heat of battle John and to follow Geneva Convention rules on taking prisoners. I have always respected this, even when we captured those murderous Taliban and Daesh fighters in the Middle-East. But I had a teenage daughter who became a drug addict......she died of an overdose just last year.....when I stood over that guy back at the house she came into my mind – she was such lovely kid – I just saw red......wrong, but it's done now.'

'Well, for sure Mac, there is no prison sentence long enough to redeem that bastard and the world must be better off without his malevolent presence'

'Christ, I don't have a clue what 'mal.......whatever' means, but I am glad you agree,'

While they were heading towards Biggin Hill Rahman called one of the Organization's London based senior operatives.

'Hi Claude, looks like the shit's flying in the West, and all of our London operatives and corrupt coppers will soon be getting arrested. We need to leave the country for some time. Look, grab the attaché case from my office, go to Park Royal for guns and ammo, and get down to Biggin Hill as soon as you can.'

'Right boss, I should be there within the hour.'

A second call was to the regular pilot of the private jet 'Graham get to the fucking airport ASAP and have the plane prepared for a long flight'

'OK boss, where are we going?'

'We will be visiting some old friends in the Lebanon....just get fucking moving'

Hanging up, Rahman was fuming – 'Why the fuck did I even get mixed up with that bitch – one day I will have her found and killed, assassins are two a penny in the Middle-East. I am just happy to have had the foresight to make regular payments over the years into various offshore accounts and the brief-case that Claude is bringing has all the details of these....so I might be exiled from Britain but it will be one spent in luxury.'

About two hours later Rahman had landed at Biggin Hill and was strapping himself into a seat in the private jet with the pilot warming up the powerful engines. Claude was sitting behind Rahman, just toying with one of the automatic rifles brought from London. The plane slowly taxied towards the end of the runway – and the pilot called up flight control 'This is aircraft Golf – Echo, Charlie, Delta, requesting permission to fly please control'

Officers in Flight control had been ordered to prevent the jet leaving Biggin Hill, if possible without alerting the fleeing criminals.

'Please just maintain your station aircraft Golf - Echo, Charlie, Delta. We will call you when we have a slot available.'

Claude had been looking out through a window of the airplane when the two BMWs came roaring over the tarmac runway towards the plane.

'Fuck boss, the bastards have caught us.'

'As big as he was, Rahman moved quickly towards the door with Claude on his heels.'

The two ran across the runway just as an airport maintenance worker was driving past on a quad-bike ....a short burst from Claude's semi-automatic saw the driver blown off the bike, and its automatic cut-off bringing the machine to a halt.

The two villains then set off on the quad-bike heading across the airport towards an exit gate.

'Shit' said John and Mac in unison.... surely we will get him eventually.'

'Who knows' said Mac. 'What we do know is that they are escaping now and we are here. I would think that the airport has more than just one quad-bike maintenance vehicle.... let's drive over to the main building and see.'

'Good call' said John

There were in fact two other quad bikes being parked in the front of the main building, fortunately they were just about to set off.

Colin flashed his warrant card but it was probably the sight of four uniformed Marines that did more to persuade the two maintenance workers to hand the bike keys over.

John and Mac, took the lead in one, with Colin and one of the Marines, following.

The chase led the bikes out of the airport perimeter and onto a footpath over farmland and then into a stretch of very muddy woodland. Rahman was driving with Claude firing his semi-automatic rifle at the two pursuing quad-bikes.

As they rounded a bend and began to climb a steep muddy hill, Claude's firing hit John in the arm making him lose control and as his quad-bike was tipping over he could see a short burst of fire from the Marine on the quad-bike at the rear hit Claude who slumped forward on to Rahman causing him to skid off the pathway, and run into the stump of a long dead oak tree – Rahman was thrown off the bike, breaking his neck as he hit an impressive stone seat in place beside the path.

With all of the quad-bikes now stopped the chasing group were gathered over the body of Ashif Rahman – Colin pointed to a carved stone plaque inset into the back of the seat that was incised with the passage:

'From Mr Wilberforce's' diary 1787

At length I well remember after a conversation with Mr Pitt in the open air at the root of an old oak tree at Holwood just above the steep descent into the Vale of Keston I resolved to give notice on a fit occasion in the House of Commons of my intention to bring forward the abolition of the slave trade'

After reading through the plaque John, Mac, and Colin stood looking down at what little now remained of the stump of the great oak that it must have been in Wilberforce's time.

'So this is where the plan for the abolition of the slave trade within the British Empire was first formulated....wow!' observed John.

'Well, how's that for irony,' said Colin.

'A bastard who ran an organisation that in effect trafficked girls into Britain to be forced into enslaved prostitution and whose drug trading activities enslaved thousands, meeting his end in collision with this memorial'

'More fucking justice than irony,' said Mac.

John seemed about to add something when he collapsed to the ground – Colin pointed at John's head 'Christ, I know he took a hit in his arm but look at that gash on his head, he must have hit it when we crashed.'

It only took about 20 minutes for John to be rushed to the local Princess Royal Hospital and two days later, when his condition had been stabilised, strings were pulled and he was transferred by military ambulance to Derriford Hospital back in Plymouth.

His recovery was steady and went well, to a considerable extent due to his mood being lifted by regular visits from Jean and Janina, who had been invited to stay at Jean's cottage.

The Met. officers had returned to London and were involved in dismantling the Organization and clearing the Met. of all the bent coppers listed in Rahman's notebook that had been retrieved, with the diamonds, from 'Sunrise'. The Marines were back in their Bickleigh base.

One week on and John was being visited by Jean when he saw Janina coming down the ward holding hands with Ben.

'So, you two have finally got together,' said John.

The love that they shared could clearly be seen in the way that the two young people gazed at each other.

'I have a present for you Janina. It is meant to serve as a reminder of what you have been through.'

This was the gift that John had bought in the Plymouth Jeweller's shop on the day Janina had been taken hostage. She opened the box and saw a predominately sky-blue enamelled broach showing a silver anchor with a gold mermaid draped around it.

Tears were running down Janina's cheeks as she looked at the broach.

'Do you remember when we first met and you were crying then...... can I ask something of you Ben....can you please put your arms around Janina'

Ben needed little encouragement, and the couple came together with some enthusiasm.

'Well Janina' said John. 'You have finally got the hug that you asked me for when you tapped on the window of my van back in Acle!'

As a postscript, let's roll the time clock on ten years.

We find Charlie and Simmo in partnership, running a very successful motor-bike sales and servicing business. Billy Macdonald, the street-level drug pusher with a conscience, has been working as their foreman mechanic for the past five years.

Harry had put himself through undergraduate and postgraduate university courses and is now a lecturer at Plymouth University.

And Ross has two more years to serve as a Captain in 42 Commando Brigade of the Royal Marines. These four had remained firm friends and when they did manage to get together the chat invariably returned to their earlier adventures.

John is married to Jean, and they have moved to a more remote part of Dartmoor where John runs his own outdoor adventure centre. And Jean is now a Chief Superintendent in the Plymouth Police Force. John's daughter Natalie often comes to stay.

They have kept in touch with Ross and are hoping that he will join the local police force when his service in the Marines comes to an end.

Janina and Ben live aboard a 40ft yacht based at a residential mooring just off the river Hamble from which they run a boat delivery service that takes them and their five year old twins on sailing voyages criss-crossing the seas.

As to Ashif Rahman and his mob, some are serving long-prison sentences and ....if there is a hell, then the rest reside there.

Milton Keynes UK
Ingram Content Group UK Ltd.
UKHW040702131024
2149UKWH00027B/134